THE

VIRGIN BRIDE.

A ROMANCE.

LONDON:

PUBLISHED BY E. LLOYD, SALISBURY-SQUARE; PURKESS
COMPTON-STREET, SOHO; AND SOLD BY ALL BOOKSELLERS.

THE VIRGIN BRIDE.

ROUGH AND READY EXAMINING THE MAP OF MEXICO.

CHAPTER I.

ROUGH AND READY IN HIS CAMP.—AN INTERVIEW WITH CAPTAIN WALKER.—A SPY IS WANTED, AND THE MAN REQUIRED IS FOUND.—THE COMMISSION.—THE DARK RIDER AND COAL-BLACK STEED.

A WORK like this needs no preface—it carries its own history along with it. If it is not written with all the beauty and force which a subject so interesting and eventful deserves, an apology certainly will not make it any more acceptable to the reader, therefore he may e'en take it as it is, and make as much of it as he chooses.

It was on the sunny morning of March 11, 1847, that the "Army of Occupation" broke up camp at Corpus Christi, preparatory to crossing the Rio Colorado, an

No. 1.

taking position on the Rio Grande, the step which hastened the present war with Mexico. Our story commences with the sunrise of this day. All of the tents save that of the commander-in-chief, had already been struck and stowed away in the baggage waggons, preparatory for a march.

Within his tent, and seated upon a rude camp stool, with a map of Mexico spread out upon his knees, was an officer, whose person, seen lithographed at every shop window in the country, scarce needs a description. It was that great general, who within a single year has won a world-wide fame, one who, whether spoken of as General Taylor, or " Old Rough and Ready," is known to all who hear the name.

Beside the general stood several of his staff, all watching the lines which he drew upon the map, for already the prospect of war was before them, and as soldiers they looked forward to a broad and ripe field in which to gather a soldier's laurels. The general was tracing along the map a line of march, which he knew would be necessary should hostilities ensue upon his crossing the Rio Colorado, as had been already threatened by the Mexicans.—With that intuitive perception of the future which has rendered Napoleon and others so remarkable, he was already planning a campaign which he knew was inevitable, and was already glancing over the ground which was soon to become the garden of his glory,

The general paused in his examination, and looking up, addressed a young officer near him.

" I wish you would have Captain Walker sent for, Major Bliss—I want him."

In a few moments a small finely-formed man, possessing a keen and flashing eye, and a face much resembling the discription which we have of South Carolina's gallant Marion, dressed in a hunting dress of the Texas Rangers, stood before the General, with his broad rimmed hat in his hand, awaiting orders.

The eye of the old general on seeing him, brightened.

" Ah, Captain Walker, I'm glad to see you. I sent for you to inquire if you have not such a man in your company as I now require for a perilous and delicate service; a duty which requires courage, tact, keen observation, retentive memory, and all of the qualities which are valuable in a spy."

" I have good men in my company, general," responded the young ranger, but I had rather go on a duty of this kind myself, than to trust others with it, sir !"

" You will not do, sir," responded the general, and then, as he saw the face of the young ranger redden, he hastened to add—" Not that I doubt either your bravery or your tact, but you are not dark enough, nor look sufficiently like a Mexican. I must have a man whose looks and knowledge of the language will enable him to pass for a native of Mexico !"

" Then sir, Charley Brackett is your man. I've not a braver man in my company; he was born and educated a gentleman, speaks Spanish perfectly, and as his mother was a Castilian, is full as dark, but not quite so yellow as a real native. If he was stained with a shade of butternut colour, and rigged up a la ranchero, he'd make as good looking a Mexican as I ever drew lead on."

' Is he faithful ; will not his Spanish blood cause him to lean toward the other side a little ?"

" If to hate the Mexicans as few can hate; if to thirst for their blood, as the desert thirsts for the dews of night ; if to live under the weight of a fearful oath to revenge an outraged mother and sister, whose corses are now mouldering in a bloody grave near San Jacinto, will ensure his faith to us, then feel secure that Charles Brackett will never prove a traitor."

" He has seen service ?"

" He fought like a demon on the field of San Jacinto. He was with me on Mier expedition, and had there been twenty more like him in our band, we never would have suffered as we did. He is now with me, waiting for the outbreak which is threatened, ready when it does come, to take a man's place, and do a man's duty."

" He will not have long to wait," said the general with a smile, and then added, you may send the young man here, sir !"

In a shore time the ranger was announced. As he entered the tent, General Taylor arose and took a calm and steady survey of the person who stood before him.

He was about five feet eight or nine inches high, with a slight but well knit figure, in which muscles seemed to make up for deficiency in size ; erect, and in form looking every inch a soldier. His age was probably about twenty-five years. His hair and eyes were of a jetty blackness, his skin was a rich brunette, his features betokened plainly his Spainish descent. There was that in his looks which showed that courage and resolution were his by nature ; and there was a certain quickness in the flash of his large eye, and the restlessness of his motions, which told that like the curbed but impetuous war-steed, he wished for action—action, the very soul and life of a true man. His weapons, the rifle, bowie knife, and a brace of revolving pistols, were in keeping with his looks.

Standing in a respectful attitude, he awaited the orders of the general, and underwent the severe and searching scrutiny without a change of look or colour.

The latter after a few moments addressed him,

" Your name is Brackett, young man, is it not?"

" Charles Brackett, general," responde the ranger.

" Your captain speaks well of you as a soldier, and recommends you as the best man in his company, and as likely to suit me for a piece of service which I have on hand."

" Captain Walker always says more for his friends than himself. I hopI may deserve his praise, but I am sure I have had no chance to do so yet."

" Young man you shall have a chance," said the general; then turning to his officers with a kind smile, he added, " Gentlemen, excuse me in requesting to be left with Major Bliss and this young man for a short time. I will join you on the march—it is time for the columns to advance."

All the officers, except Major Bliss, left the tent.

General Taylor seated himself, and calling the ranger to his side, spread the map out before him and again opened the conversation.

" You have already been in Mexico, and seen service," said he.

" I have, but I hope that the day of my service is but just dawning, for what I have done, like the smell of blood to the famishing tiger, only excites my thirst for more."

" Look upon this map, Mr. Brackett. Follow that pencil mark to the mouth of the Rio Grande, then up its banks to Matamoras. Let your eye mark each point."

" I do mark them, general."

" Very well, sir, now follow up the river—how high can it be navigated with steam boats ?"

" To Camargo—I crossed it not far from that point when we were on our route to Mier."

" Very well, sir—now which think you is the most direct route from Camargo to Mexico ?"

" I have never been beyond Camargo on the lower route, but I think that from there, about south-west, or a few degrees more westerly, to Monterey, then south-west, a little westerly to Saltillo, thence south to San Luis Potosi, would be the nearest and most passable way."

" You are right, young man, quite right—I've marked out this very route; and now, sir, you shall know the service I require. It is probable that we shall have to travel this path before long. I wish the route examined, the state of the country carefully noted. I wish to know the condition of the fortifications ; the prospects for obtaining water and supplies of provisions on the road ; in short, sir, I wish to know everything which would be useful to me in case of a war of invasion becoming necessary."

" I am ready to perform this duty, sir," responded the ranger, readily, " but disguise will be necessary. I am well known to many Mexicans, yes, they have known me as I have known them—to their sorrow."

"You must, of course, disguise yourself as a Mexican—you will receive funds and all other things that you require by applying to Major Bliss."

"How far do you wish me to penetrate into the country?"

"At present no farther than Saltillo and the passes of the mountains near there, on the road to San Luis Potosi. Do this and return with all speed, for we may be at work before you come back, and your arm may be needed here?"

"I will go and return in twenty-five days, general, if you give me funds to freshen my supply of horse-flesh now and then, for I am a hard rider."

"Major Bliss will furnish all you require," responded the general, smiling at the last remark of the young ranger, and then he added; the sooner you are fixed and in the saddle, the better, for time is precious!"

"I will be on my route in an hour, general," responded the ranger, and as he spoke he hastily left the tent.

"I like that youngster, Major Bliss, promptness is a great virtue in a soldier's character," said the general, when he and his adjutant were left alone.

"It made Napoleon, and the want of it has lost many a noble opportunity to other generals!" was the brief reply of one who says but little, but thinks a great deal, Major W. W. S. Bliss.

The general responded not to this remark, but looking at his watch, changed the tenor of the conversation by remarking that it was time he was in the saddle. Then hastily folding up his pocket map, he deposited it in a breast pocket of his old blue surtout, and left the tent.

One hour afterward the head of the advance column was passed by a man at full speed, well mounted on a fleet and heavily built black horse. The rider was dressed completely a la banchero. At his saddle hung the ever useful lasso; a short rifled carbine was slung over his back; holsters were in their places, and though closely covered with oil-cloth to protect their contents from the weather, no one would doubt after a single glance at the rider, that the weapons were within and ready for use. A short sabre or machete was suspended from his belt, in which was also placed a brace of revolvers, which, however, were hidden from sight by the neat poncho, or Mexican blanket which he wore carelessly over his shoulder. His legs were cased in the wide trowsers of the country; upon his boots, made of untanned hide, he wore a pair of spurs heavy enough to tire a common leg to carry them, the rowels being at least an inch in length, the chains and braces in proportion. From beneath a broad rimmed Panama hat, peered a pair of flashing black eyes, and these were set in a face complexioned much like a bright chocolate colour, though near two thirds of it were hidden in a moustache and beard so long, black, curling and glossy, that even Charley May would have envied a beard so oriental, so perfectly *magnifique*. As the rider passed by the column and rode along the flank of Rangers, who as scouts led the way, he cast a fierce looking glance at them, and as he twisted the end of his jetty moustache, he spoken no gentle tones.

"Malditos Americanos! A dote vas, bijos de infierne?" "Cursed Americans. Where are you going, you sons of hell?" and as some who understood the language answered in language full as coarse and scornful, he burst out with a wild and contemptuous laugh, and dashed on, as he turned for the last time to look upon them, 'froco—froco!' an expression equivalent to saying wait a little time!'

Little did those hardy rangers dream that in that fierce and vindictive looking Mexican was their especial favourite, Charley Brackett, he who in the field was reckoned the bravest and most expert of them all in their guerilla mode of warfare.

As Brackett rode on out of their hearing, he checked his horse down into a speed which, though rapid, would not over-tax his power, and, as he kept on in a laughing soliloquy, he expressed his pleasure at the completeness of a disguise which had blinded the eagle eyes of his most intimate comrades.

It was indeed necessary that he should be well disguised, for many a Mexican had heard his battle-shout, many a fugitive from the strife of blood had as he turned rein from the battle-field, seen the flash of his jet black eye, and heard the crash of his sabre as it dealt out death to those who were more tardy than he in flight.

Yes, there was one, who now held rank in the Mexican army, who had twice almost miraculously escaped from the revengeful hand of the son and brother whose home he had made desolate, and Colonel Gustave Alfrede would have given half his weight in gold to know of the death of young Brackett, for he had heard of the "oath of revenge" and he knew but too well that while Charles Brackett lived his own life was in as much danger as if he walked through a prairie stocked with deadly serpents.

On through the warm, sunny day, over the broad and bright savannas and through the occasional chapparal, pressed that coal black steed and his rider, on swiftly to fulfil his dangerous, but important mission.

CHAPTER II.

BUENA VISTA.—A DESCRIPTION OF THE OWNER OF THE HACIENDA AND HIS FAMILY. DONNA MAGDALENA INTRODUCED, ALSO THE BEAUTIFUL XIMENA.—COLONEL ALFREDE, A SUITOR.—A MOONLIGHT RIDE.—A SONG.—AND BRACKETT, THE RANGER.

A BEAUTIFUL place is that which has lately become so noted as "the bloody field of Buena Vista;" a spot which took its name from the grand and romantic view which it presented. Reader, see a valley which hangs in evergreen beauty between a range of dark and lofty mountains; not a level monotonous plain, but a beautiful "rolling" country, interspersed here and there with little hills, pretty groves, rushing rivulets which supply the channel of the little river San Juan, which flows along the western side of the valley. Springs like blue spots in a white-cloud-mottled-sky, are seen here and there; in some parts of it fields of green and broad leafed corn are waving in the breeze; in others herds of cattle are grazing, or lolling in the shade of luxuriant trees; while here and there may be seen some lazy labourer attending to his duties on the hacienda.

You see that stone house on the Saltillo road; it is built like a castle, has its watchtower and battlements, and is built of the dark, reddish stone which the hills on either side display.

That building is the residence of Don Ignatio Valdez, the owner of the hacienda or estate of Buena Vista. We enter it reader, and pay Don Ignatio and his family a visit.

Don Ignatio is a Castilian noble, he left his country about ten years since, in consequence of the failure of the attempts which Don Carlos made to gain the throne of Spain. Ignatio was in heart, aye in very soul a Carlist. He was a cotemporary with Zumelacarraguei, the greatest guerilla chieftain who ever led men forth at dead of night to form the quiet ambuscade, or defend the narrow mountain pass; but Zumelacarraguei fell, and with him the hopes of Don Carlos.

Then Don Ignatio sought domestic happiness and quiet in this beautiful valley, and here he buried SEBERINA, his wife; the better angel of his early days; the living MEMORY of his ripened life.

But when she left the cares of life for the joys of heaven, he was not alone. Two fair daughters, Magdalena and Ximena were left unto him to soften down the grief which might have overwhelmed even his stern soul.

The first—and, reader, she will soon be better known to you—was, at the time when our visit is made, a girl of sweet seventeen, but one who seemed several years in advance of her age;—not that she looked old, but her manners, and grace, and accomplishments, were beyond her years. Let me describe her.

She is above the medium height; yet her form is so full so perfectly proportioned, that she does not look too tall ; her low-necked dress reveals shoulders that are graceful as a sculptor's ideal, and a neck which Canova would have copied; her bare arms are round, full, and taper beautifully down to a dear little hand, which looks as if it was only made to hold the most delicate flowers of nature. Her face bespeaks a warm and enthusiastic heart, for she has a large beaming eye of jetty blackness ; lips full and rosy ; cheeks which, though quite brunette, are transparent as the rind of the pomegranate. Her eye-brows are arched as the moon on its birth night, her features are as classic as Salvator Rosa's beautiful Madona ; her hair is like waves of curled silk :—and this, reader, is the heroine of our story. Oh! well was she known to all the noble cavaliers of Saltillo—and even as far as the golden city of the Montezumas—as the beautiful " Maiden of Buena Vista !" In disposition she was gay and dashing—much like the " Die Vernon" of Walter Scott.

Her sister Ximena was a different being, both in person and character. The latter was a delicate, fragile flower of humanity, a kind of fairy in appearance. Though one year older than her sister she was small, delicately formed, more pale than the other, and so quiet and dreamy in her ways, that she had gained among those who knew her the name of " La Pensarosa," or " The Sentimental." Her features were fully indicative of her Castilian origin ; her eye, however, was not flashing and bright, like her sister's, but soft, dewy and soulfull.

So much for the daughters—now for their father. The hair of Don Ignatio, or what little he had left, for he was nearly bald, was white as the snows which cap Orizabo's mighty peak ; his features were of a Roman cast, and his face wore that look of habitual dignity which seems so natural to a Castilian. His form, though it bore the weight of near sixty winters, was firm and erect ; his step had all the elasticity of youth, and his voice, when he spoke to his well-loved children was soft as the voice of a troubadour. He ever wore his sword, and had a hand not only ready, but able to use the weapon, which had been the plaything of his boyhood, the companion of his whole life. If he had a fault, it was that he too much adored his two children. He was open-hearted, liberal to an extreme, and though once blessed with a considerable fortune, so careless of it had he been, that he was now involved in embarrassments ; and even Buena Vista, his beautiful estate, was only held under a mortgage, the interest of which he scarce could meet.

These pecuniary troubles were excessively mortifying to his pride ; yet Don Ignatio managed to keep his place in society, and to keep an " open house" for his friends.

Among those, the military were predominant, in consequence of the tastes which he had imbibed with his early life ; and it of course will seem quite natural that soldiers, who, like sailors, are ever warm admirers of beauty, would flock to the house of Don Ignatio, as bees gather unto a flower-garden.

Of course the young ladies found plenty of admirers. Of these none was more attentive than one Colonel Alfrede, to Magdalena. The colonel was a man of rather prepossessing appearance, whose age might be thirty, but not more. He was rich, commanded a regiment of lancers, and had a reputation for gallantry both in the battle-field and ladies' boudoirs, which rendered him quite an object of envy to his brother officers, and a subject of fear to such Mexican husbands in his vicinity as had young, gay and pretty wives.

Strange to say, this good-looking and very redoubtable officer could produce no impression on the heart of Donna Magdalena. She scarce knew why, yet she felt an unconquerable repugnance to him. Her father favoured the suit of Alfrede, for the latter had always seemed to him to be very noble and generous. Repeatedly he had unasked proffered loans to him, when those loans were very acceptable ; and he had never had the impertinence to assume the character of a dun. Don Ignatio had, almost unawares to himself, become indebted to Alfrede for several thousand dollars ; and this perchance added to his willingness to have him for a son-in-law. But Donna Magdalena used every effort to avoid even meeting the colonel, and when in his company, took but little trouble to conceal her distaste for it.

At the time when our history commences, this officer was so busily engaged in preparing his regiment for service, according to the orders of his government, that she was in a measure relieved from his odious attentions.

His quarters were in Saltillo, about seven miles north of her father's place. He used, as often as he could withdraw himself from his duties, to ride out to Buena Vista, generally accompanied by an escort of his lancers, more for show than use, for as yet Buena Vista was a valley of peace and quiet.

We have now introduced the reader to Don Ignatio and his family, and made him partially acquainted with the situation of its members.

Without following the course of Charles Brackett from the American camp, we will slide quietly over the space of a few days, which were to him barren of adventure, and meet him at the "*Pasado del Estrangeros*," or hotel of the strangers, which stands fronting the Plaza in the city of Saltillo. He had come thus far without discovery, had carefully reconnoitred Monterey and all of the points which were embraced in his orders, and had now nearly reached the farthest point of his travels. This was a source of pleasure to him, for already had the news overtaken him of General Taylor's arrival at the Rio Grande, and from the "curses loud and deep," which he heard around him, and took good care to echo, he knew that war was inevitable, and he sighed to return in time to take a leading hand in the first game.

It was night when he arrived in Saltillo—a clear and beautiful evening. He had his horse carefully groomed immediately on his arrival at the hotel, and then partook of a hasty supper, after which he intended to take a walk round the town and reconnoitre its position and defences. But on coming out into the open air, and finding it to be a clear, moonlight evening, he determined to hire a fresh horse and ride a few miles farther on, as he had been directed, so that he might be able to retrace his route on the next day. He easily procured a steed, and rode on toward the mountain gorges, which he had been directed to examine.

His path led directly past the house of Don Ingnatio, where he was passing carelessly, when a voice so rich and full fell upon his ear, that he involuntary reined in his steed, and stopped to listen.

He caught but one verse of the song, which seemed to be a simple, but exceedingly sweet Spanish air.

The verse which he heard was peculiar. Here it is.

> " 'Tis true that I'm living in maidenly leisure
> With nothing to vex or cross me me in my pleasure,
> But a dear little husband far better would be,
> Oh, a dear little husband were treasure to me."

When Brackett heard this song in tones rich and lively, as if the singer cared very little about having the boon which in her happy ignorance, she pronounces ' a treasure,' he remembered it as one he had heard years before from the lips of his loved sister, and prompted by he knew not what, he followed the song by adding the next verse, but simply altering the masculine terminations into the feminine, so as to make the song apply to a wish for a dear little wife—thus :

> " 'Tis true I've a bachelor's life all before me,
> My father is easy, my mother adores me,
> But a dear little wife how much better would be.
> Oh a dear little wife were a treasure to me."

As his clear voice arose in this pretty cadenza, he looked up to the window casement whence he had heard the voice of the female, and caught one quick glance at a beautiful face, which seemed full of fun and mischief, as it glanced out in the moonlight to catch a glimpse of him. The eyes of both the singers met, but hers was in an instant withdrawn, and the next moment the swinging lattie of the window was closed.

Brackett looked for another view of her face in vain, and after waiting for moment, he rode on, murmuring as he passed—'beautiful as an angel.' Perhaps she heard his words, at any rate, a sweet musical laugh fell upon his ear from behind that lattice immediately after.

Putting spurs to his horse, he dashed rapidly along the road ; but that voice seemed to follow him wherever he went, he could not banish it from his mind. Ere midnight was past, he had completed his reconnoitre, and returned to the city.   In passing the mansion at Buena Vista on his return, he paused and tried to get another glimpse of the fair singer, but he paused in vain. All was still. She was probably revelling amid the joys of dream-land.

" She was beautiful !" he exclaimed, as he rode towards the city. Little dreamed he that he had met Magdalena Valdez, one who was reputed the fairest maiden in all Mexico, yet much he pondered as he rode back to his hotel, whether he should ever meet her again.   Perhaps he thought how horrible would be the scenes of war to such as she, and almost shuddered while he thought to what dangers a war exposed beautiful maidens and helpless women.

CHAPTER III.

THE RECOGNITION OF THE RANGER.—THE PURSUIT.—THE DEATH OF THE PUR-
SUING LANCERS.— THE RANGER IS CAPTURED, HIS LIFE PRESERVED BY THE
BEAUTIFUL MAGDALENA.

It was but a little after sun-rise. Donna Magdalena and her sister Ximena stood at the same window which she had been seated at, when Charles Brackett had passed on the previous evening, and heard her sing.

And he was the subject of their conversation.

" Who could he be ? I thought that I knew, by sight at least, all of the noble cavaliers within leagues of Buena Vista—and he was so handsome, so manly in his bearing. Oh, sister, you know not what you have lost by retiring to your bed so early. You should have seen him and heard him !"

This was the effect which the single glance that she had caught of the ranger produced upon Donna Magdalena   Her sister laughed as she listened to her earnest tone, and cried :

" I think you must have given your heart to that unknown stranger, sister ; I never before heard you say so much for a man !" replied the other.

" I never before saw a man who appeared to me to be worth saying so much for !" replied the other.

" What did he look like —did he resemble Colonel Alfrede ?"

" Oh, why do you mention that hated name, Ximena ? The stranger looked so much more noble than he, as looks the proud war-steed nobler than the crop-eared shaggy pack-mule !"

" Well, that is a comparison, indeed.''

" Yet, methinks it suits very well ;—truth will often make similar comparisons —I am sure there are as many asses with two legs in the world, as there are four-legged ones.''

" Perhaps more—but look, sister—look toward the city ! See that cloud of dust. Surely Alfrede is not coming with his lancers to breakfast with us !"

" Heaven forfend the infliction of his presence," cried the other, quickly glancing in the direction pointed out by her sister, and then she exclaimed, " What may it mean? I can see horsemen riding at full speed this way. Get the little field-glass that father used to carry in Spain, Ximena, it will enable us to discern the objects plainer !"

The elder sister hastened to get the glass, and in a moment Magdalena was looking up the Saltillo through it.

"What see you, sister?" asked Ximena, as she saw the face of the sister flush up with excitement.

"I see a large company of Alfrede's lancers; They ride this way—they seem to be in pursuit of one who rides upon a coal-black horse. They are close upon him, but he rides with the speed of the wind. Ha—he turns his steed in the road, and pauses. He fires a shot from his gun, and the foremost lancer falls from his horse. Oh! what may it mean?"

MAGDALENA SAVES THE LIFE OF CHARLES BRACKETT.

"Perhaps it is some robber escaping—look again, sister, and tell me what you see."

"He again speeds swiftly down the road—they seem to close upon him—his horse looks worn—ha! he fires a pistol—another lancer falls—another, and yet another—four are down! They fire at him, yet he still rides on, as if unarmed! He must be a demon to stand that volley. Ah, he stoops in his saddle—he must be wounded—but no! he comes on, on, swifter than before. The lancers follow close in his rear."

No. 2.

" Is Alfrede there ?"

" Yes, I see him ; but he is not in the front of his company—but the pursued. Oh, how rash ! he pauses again—he has loaded his gun, it was for that he stooped in his saddle.　He raises his piece—he fires—Oh, Ximena ! I am free from persecution ; Alfrede falls, thank God for that shot !"

" Oh no, sister, it cannot be—give me the glass !" cried the other ; and she now became the watcher of the scene.

" Is it not so, has he not fallen ?" asked Magdalena.

" No, he is up again ; it was only his horse that was shot ; he dismounts one of his lancers, and takes his horse and pursues,　The pursued is coming near very fast.　His black horse is becoming white with foam.　That rider looks like a noble cavalier ; may be it is your stranger of last night, and Alfrede is jealous of him, and wishes to destroy him !"

Ximena spoke in jest ; but little dreamed she how near the truth she came.

The sister started, as she heard this remark, and again taking the glass, looked forth.　Her cheek paled as she looked—her whole form quivered, and her voice trembled, as in a husky whisper, she said—

" It is—it is !　Oh, God grant he may escape.　See, he fires his pistol again and another lancer falls.　Alfrede is encouraging the others to follow, and leads them now with his drawn sword flashing in his hand.　The stranger's horse reels, he is bleeding.　The rider, too, is wounded.　Oh God, save him !—but why do I feel this strange interest ?"

The scene was now rapidly approaching Buena Vista.　The ranger, for it was Bracket who was pursued, was urging on his steed towards the house, and already was he near it.　Donna Magdalena, wild with terror and excitement, rushed from her chamber, down into the open court she sped, and out to the gate of the dwelling. Ximena, of a frailer nature, fainted in the chamber.　Don Ignatio was not in the house ; he was absent somewhere on the plantation.　At the moment Donna Magdalena reached the gate, she saw the horse of the stranger, who was within an hundred yards of the house, fall dead upon the ground.　The rider pressed on— but his steps showed that he was weak and wounded.　The lancers were close upon him, and Alfrede was at their head.　The beautiful girl rushed forward—but ere she could reach the side of Brackett, Alfrede had struck a sweeping blow with his sabre, aimed full at the head of the ranger.　The latter had received the blow upon his sword ; but the blade of the weapon snapped near the hilt, and he was defenceless.　At this instant, as he fell fainting to the ground, Magdalena sprang before him, and while she looked upon Alfrede and his men a scorn which she could not speak, she cried :

" Cowards ! would you strike a fallen foe ?　Back, if ye are men !　What has this stranger done, that ye seek his life ?"

" He is a traitor—a Texan !" shouted some of the band ; but their colonel, respectfully dropping the point of his sword, in a gentler tone, said—

" Donna Magdalena, this is no place for you—this man must be my prisoner !" Then turning to his men he added, " Harm him not at present, but secure him— he shall be properly tried before a court-martial, though to do so but renders his fate quite as certain."

" What fate—surely he must not die simply because he is an enemy, and has fallen into your power?　And besides, he cannot be a Texan ; he is of your own nation.　Look at him ; his face, garb and all, tell it !"

The Colonel smiled as he removed from the fallen man, the false beard and moustache, which covered his face ; and then the maiden gazed with wonderment, and increased anguish, as she saw that he was young, and more handsome without than with his beard.

" Is he badly wounded ?" she asked, as she saw the officer examine the wounds.

" No ; very slightly—nothing but flesh wounds, which have wasted his blood so much as to weaken him—nothing more.　I shall have to use your father's house for a prison, however, until to-morrow, when I can remove him to the city for trial."

The maiden seemed pleased at this idea, and made no objection to having him borne into the house.

The reader is, doubtless, anxious to know how the ranger's disguise became penetrated, and his discovery made. We will gratify him.

On rising in the morning at the Posada, and ordering his horse, he saw that the Plaza was occupied by a regiment of lancers at drill, and he stood for some time at the door, watching their evolutions. He did not observe an officer who stood near him, whose eye was not upon the lancers, but upon himself. That eye was scanning him with a dangerous scrutiny—that officer was Gustave Alfrede, the murderer of his mother and sister—the perpetrator of that nameless crime upon them, which sinks all other crimes into nothingness. He had recognised the ranger, and was now thinking how he could get him into his power, with the least danger to himself, for he knew that he was ever in danger while his foe lived ; he knew of the "oath of revenge"—an oath sworn over the bodies of those whom he had violated and slain.

After a few moments of delay, carelessly spent in watching the drill of the lancers, Brackett mounted his horse, and started to ride around and examine the city, turning his horse's head toward the south gate. He had scarcely got into his saddle, when he saw an officer pass out from the inn, mount a horse, which was held by a soldier near the door, and dash at full speed across the Plaza, to the head of the body of lancers.

The ranger, at a single glance, recognised his enemy—he saw him speak to the lancers and point towards him ; and then he knew that he was recognised. His first thought was to turn, and single handed, meet the foe ; his next told him how important his mission was to his country—and he put spurs to his horse, followed at full speed by the shouting lancers. His horse was tired with a weary route of travel, but the noble animal bounded off, at first, with a speed which threatened soon to leave pursuit behind ; but ere five miles were passed, he began to flag, and soon the foe came within shot of the ranger. The reader knows the rest of the adventure, up to the moment of the capture.

CHAPTER IV.

INTERVIEW BETWEEN ALFREDE AND DON IGNATIO. —THE MORTGAGE, AND THREAT. BRIBING A MEXICAN SOLDIER.—DONNA MAGDALENA AND THE PRISONER.—PLAN OF ESCAPE.

It was midnight, and Don Ignatio Valdez was closeted with Colonel Alfrede in his private chamber. The prisoner was confined in a lower room of the Casa, with a guard of two soldiers over him, while all the rest of the lancers had been sent to their quarters in the city.

It was midnight, the end of the day which had commenced with his capture. The reader is permitted to listen to the conversation of Don Ignatio and his companion, in order that he may have a full comprehension of the situation and intentions of all parties.

"Don Ignatio, it seems to me that a little more of your parental authority, a little more severity of manner, might at least induce her to treat me with common respect."

" Don Gustave, she is wild and wilful, I know ; but Magdalena has never heard a harsh word from my lips, and it is hard for me to begin now, when each day renders her, if possible, more and more dear to me !"

"I ask you not to speak harshly to her, Don Ignatio; I only ask you to advise her to treat me with more respect—more kindness—not as if I were a slave, unworthy of a kind word, or a smile."

"I will talk to her, Don Gustave. You know how desirous I am that she should be pleased with you—how desirous I am to have her accept your proffered suit—if you will only be patient, her repugnance to yourself will wear away, and all will yet be as you desire."

"Patience, senor! patience itself can be worn out. I have wooed your daughter for three years—aye, sought with all the devotion of my heart to please and win her affections. By her daily conduct, you can see how I have prospered—and still, sir, you say have patience!"

This was spoken in a tone so impatient, that it somewhat touched the pride of the Castilian noble, and he haughtily answered—

"You need not expect to use force, sir, to win her love or her hand. The daughter of a Valdez has a heart which can never he chained, save by its own consent!"

The Colonel saw that he had been rather hasty, and in a milder tone, said —

"Pardon me, Don Ignatio; I mean not that force was required — yet methinks a kind father's words of persuasion would be influential with a daughter ever dutiful, as is Donna Magdalena. Pardon me, if I have urged too strongly my suit. A passion so deep and fervent as mine, is like the swollen torrent which rushes down yon mountain's side; cheek or dam its course, and it will swell beyond the bank which should confine it."

"You are pardonable, certainly; Don Gustave; the more so, that your present nature is so much like mine at your age. I will speak to the girl; I will urge your claims?" said Don Ignatio, who with his generous disposition was quite as easily pacified as angered, and as he said this, he bowed and left the apartment.

"Yes, for your own sake you had better urge my claims upon the proud girl; aye, and for her's! Little dreams she, or little thinks he that I own the roof which shelters them—the domain that surrounds them. The mortgage is mine, and one act of mine would drive them forth, or even make peons of them all!"

This was the soliloquy of Alfrede, uttered as Don Ignatio left the room, and the last threat was a fearful one; for it is a common custom to sell a debtor in Mexico, until by his labour for a term of years he pays his debt, and there are authentic instances where such a slavery has been contracted for life.

It was the same hour. In a small room near the opening of the court of Don Ignatios house, lay Charles Brackett. sleeping upon a rough settee, which had been before time used as a resting place for the porter, whose apartment it was.

He slept soundly, as if fatigue had overcome him. Though his face was a little pale, still his breathings were sufficiently heavy to show that his wounds had not left him in a dangerous situation. The bandages and dressings which were applied looked clumsy and awkward, as if applied by some hand unused to attending to wounds. The regular step of the sentinel in front of the door did not serve to disturb him—like those who have become used to danger and peril, he cared little apparently for the situation in which he was placed, even though he knew himself to be at the mercy of an inveterate foe. Besides, he had been worn down with the toil he had undergone, having been constantly in the saddle for many days, and all this left him but little disposed for wakefulness.

The sentinel was almost as drowsy, and as he leaned against the door-post at the intervals when he paused in his walk, he would yawn and exhibit other somnambulic symptoms.

It was twelve, and he had yet another hour to watch, before the time when he could wake his relief, who lay upon his poncho, asleep, in the entrance of the court. We know not whether the sentinel believed in ghosts or not, but he started very much and trembled violently as he saw the door of an apartment which led from the centre of the building opened, and a figure dressed in white silently advance toward him. He did not tremble quite so much as the figure came nearer, and he recognised in it the form of Donna Magdalena, and he bowed respectfully as she approached. On her arm she bore a basket, which, as it was uncovered, exhibited a tempting display to one who belonged to a proverbially ill-fed army. There was wine, bread, meat, and fruit.

While he placed himself in front of the door, the soldier looked wistfully down into the basket, and though by his position he showed that the lady could pass by farther, still his his manner betokened a respect, which possibly might have been heightened by the contents of her basket.

" The prisoner has not had any food or wine yet ; I have brought him, some," said the lady, as she approached.

" My orders, Senorita, are not to admit———"

" You have no orders not to admit refreshments to him, surely," said the lady, interrupting him, and then as she saw the direction in which his eyes involuntarily wandered, she added—" I knew that you must be fatigued with your long watching. I have brought a bottle of wine for you, and also some food !"

The soldier's eyes sparkled as he heard this welcome piece of information, but he moved not from before the door which he guarded.

The lady stooped, and taking the bottle of wine and other articles which she had brought for him, set them upon the end of a rude bench which was placed at one side of the door, and then, with a beautiful smile, she said :—

" Surely you will not refuse to let a helpless foe share in the necessary refreshment to sustain life—that would be unlike a cavalier, very unlike a true-hearted soldier !"

" Lady, I wish that I dared to please you in this, but my orders are to admit no one, not even to unbar the door myself."

" I will unbar it for you—you need not see me enter, you surely need not fear that he will escape. He is too weak."

" Lady, I fear not that—but my orders———"

" Your orders, you say, are not to unbar that door to any one—now, do you sit down on that bench and partake of the refreshments which I know you need. Sit with your back to the door, then I can give the poor prisoner some food, and you will neither unbar the door nor see it done. You know that he cannot escape— you see that you will not transgress your orders. All are sleeping in the house— this is an act of Christian mercy, and such acts are seldom seen—you need not fear.

The soldier tried to look sternly—but the lady smiled very sweetly—and then she put out her small white hand, and laying it upon his rude shoulder, pushed him very gently toward the bench where lay the food and wine. Her touch was so light that it would not have crushed a flower, yet, strange to say, it moved the stalwart guard from before the door. She led him to the bench, and when she seated him, smiled sweetly and said—" Now don't look around—I will give him the refreshments and soon return !"

" Maldit! but she is a queen—and this wine is very good !" muttered the soldier as he took breath after a hearty draught of the latter. He then proceeded to " lay in" the more substantial articles, taking particular care not to turn his eyes toward the door.

We again enter the prison, if such we may term the room wherein Brackett was sleeping. When Magdalena went in she saw that he was asleep, and setting her basket upon the floor she cautiously approached his side.

Long and ardently she gazed down into his manly face, and then murmured ;—

" So young—so handsome—and yet Alfrede says he must die ! No ! it must not—shall not be so. What if he is a Texan? he was taken in arms, and he shall not be murdered !"

Again she bent her head down to his brow, and impressed a warm, pure kiss upon it. He moved slightly as she did this, and in his sleep murmered ; " Mother, —sister !" Oh, where were then his dreams? Had the dream-spirit borne him back to his boyish days of happiness ? Oh, what a blessed power has a good Providence placed within our minds ; that of permitting it in sleep to return to scenes of joy that are past and gone for ever ; that of dreaming that we still hold communication with loved departed ones. There is an angel up in heaven who often comes down to me in dreams, and when my spirit almost faints with the toils of this world, she whispers cheering words, and tells me that the hour of rest is approaching. Oh, bless God, for the power of dreaming!

But to return from our involuntary digression. When Magdalena heard these words, she seemed to feel that none save a mother or sister held sway in his heart, for one ever whispers his dearest secrets in dreams; and again she pressed her lips to his brow, perhaps more fervently than before, for the touch awoke him. For an instant he seemed unable to recognize her, or comprehend her presence, but the confusion of awakening passed, and he was about to speak.

Quick as thought, Magdalena laid her finger upon his lips, and whispered:

"Be silent, senor! Your life is in danger—yes, he has said that you must die! But I will save you. Are you strong enough to ride!"

"I know not," he answered in the same low tone; "I am very weak, but if once in the saddle, I think it would still take trouble to unhorse me!"

"Another day would strengthen you much, would it not?"

"Not if as to-day, I am left without care or nourishment."

"Ah, I had forgotten! I have brought you wine and food!"

She hastened to administer these, and after the cup of wine he seemed much strengthened. His colour heightened, and without much effort he raised himself to a sitting posture.

"I am better, lady—and I now remember that to you I owe my life. It is not worth much to me, yet I truly feel grateful to you, who are a stranger!"

"Senor, I did but my duty to a fellow creature. I would do more—I would save you from your present peril!"

"What is that peril?"

"Colonel Alfrede says that you are a traitor—that you must die!"

"He! he knows that if I live he must die! he, the murderer, the worse than murderer of my mother and sister!"

"Your mother and sister!—those of whom you but now whispered in your dreams. Did he murder them?"

"Yes, lady—after committing that nameless wrong which would render life itself a curse to a virtuous woman! He slew them, and their bones lie beneath the plains of Texas. I have sworn to revenge the fearful wrong—if I live, that oath shall be accomplished!"

The maiden shuddered as she heard those low-tone, thrilling words—and turned pale as she gazed upon his flushed face, and saw how flashed his jet black eye; but she answered—

"You shall live, senor! Gustave Alfrede is my persecutor—my enemy too!"

"Then, lady, we are friends, even by the hate we hold!"

The lady's blush was deeper still, as she answered—

"We will be friends—but you must fly from here!"

"How can I?—My horse was ruined in this morning's skirmish."

"My father has fleet horses in his stable—but another thought strikes me. Alfrede has the fleetest horse in the country. You shot his usual road horse that morning, and he sent for his favorite war-horse. It is now in the stable—but I fear you are too weak to ride at once?"

"I am used to the saddle, let me be once seated in it, and I can long sustain myself there!"

"I think another day can be gained, and that will revive you. It will give you strength to make a forced march, which will take you beyond his reach."

"How can this delay be caused?"

"Feign excessive weakness. I will be more complaisant to him than usual—and thus easily prevail on him to delay for another day your removal to the city, where you will be court-martialed. To-morrow night all shall be ready for your flight."

"But my guards?"

"I have conquered one of them with a bottle of wine—to-morrow night he shall have another, but it shall be drugged! All shall be prepared, fear not!"

"Lady, how can I repay for all this kindness?"

"By not forgetting Magdalena Valdez when you return to your own country; and if as I fear, there should come war with all its horrors upon my country, and you should be among our foes, if you are kind to the helpless, then will I be repaid!

"Lady, I will never forget you—and I will spare all who fall within my power save him—but when I meet Gustave Alfrede, he must die!"

She smiled sadly, and simply said—

"He is my foe too!"

"He shall not long live to persecute you, lady, but beware of him, and be ever on your guard!"

"I surely should not fear him!" said she, as she showed the pearl hilt of a dagger, which she carried in her bosom, and then she added, "remember to feign entire exhaustion on the morrow. You shall have more wine and food sent you in the mean time, and be ready to-morrow night. Your weapons, or others, shall be ready for you, and I will make your escape sure!"

Ere he could answer her, she had left the room.

"Beautiful as an angel, and kind as——as a woman!" said the prisoner when he looked around, and then he added, in a tone which was anything but lover-likee "yet after all she is a Mexican—one of that cursed nation whom I have swor, to hate!"

When Donna Magdalena came out from the prisoner's room, she found the gaurd still engaged at the employment in which she had left him. Barring the door as she had found it, she approached him, and handing him a piece of gold, sa d—

"The prisoner is very low and weak—he seems hardly to have life in him!'

"I should think he wouldn't have much, after all the blood that was let out o' his veins; I'm sure I wouldn't," said the soldier, and then looking round, he askedf "Is the door barred, lady?"

"Yes," she replied, "it is just as I found it. Be careful not to have this visit known to your colonel—you will be no loser by your discretion!"

"I shall be careful, for my own sake, if for no other," said the soldier, and the next moment the lady was gone bearing with her the basket and bottles, to prevent discovery.

CHAPTER V.

PALO ALTO AND RESACA DE LA PALMA.—MAY'S CHARGE.—THE RETURN OF BRACKETT, ECT.

IT was a hot and sultry day, that of the eighth of May, 1846. Our troops were on the march with a train of provisions and artillery, from Point Isabel to Foit Brown; General Taylor commanding in person.

The troops were much excited. They had heard by the signal guns from the fort, that it was surrounded on the previous day, and now that not a gun was heard from that direction, they were left to fear that the gallant Brown and h's brave companions, had fought in vain against overpowering numbers. Under these feelings they pressed rapidly on, but ere noon their advanced scouts reported that the enemy were in front in large force, and that though the day was then hot, it was like to be hotter ere it closed. At two o'clock they found themselves beside small stream, in front of a grove, which from its tall timbers was called Palo Alto, a name which is written in letters of blood in our history. Here they saw the enemy before them, and here they paused to fill their canteens with water, and to prepare for the fearful struggle which was soon to commence. While the line of battle was forming immediately under the supervision of "Old Rough and Ready," Lieutenant Blake made a most gallant reconnoisance of the enemy's line, and as soon as his report was made to General Taylor, the action commenced. First the fire of the Mexican batteries opened, then ours returned the salute, while steadily and firmly our whole line pressed on to meet them. But we need not give a history of this battle. Enough has already been written of it to sicken the reader. Oh, it was a glorious and yet a fearful sight. Cavalry wheeling here and there; cannon pouring out their iron hail upon masses of infantry, which melted before the tremendous fire, as snow flakes falling into the sea; lances and sabres meeting and clashing; bayonet to bayonet, and breast to breast; on the open prairie and in the dense chapparal, thus met the foes, gallantly fighting, and all, too, thickly falling. Here fell Ringgold and Page, and many of those gallant souls who are nameless on the page of history, because they were privates!

Oh, it was a sad and harrowing sight to see so many human beings lay mangled upon the bosom of their mother earth; yet the sun went down upon it. The armies had ceased through fatigue, and the approach of darkness. Under cover of this cloak, the enemy retired to a more defensible spot, whereon to renew the fight once more.

Few slept that night of all our little army, though they were permitted to lay down upon the tentless ground, with their arms beneath them ready for instant use.

Their general neither lay down or closed his eyes. Beside a small camp-fire beneath a clump of trees, upon a fallen tree-trunk, receiving the reports of the different officers, and giving orders preparatory to resuming his march in the morning, he sat, calm as if the fatigues of the day, and the peril of the fight, had made no impression upon him. True, his face flushed and his breast heaved, when he heard that Ringgold and Page must die; but he grew calm again when he thought that the battle was but half won, and must be resumed with the morning's light.

It was after midnight, when he arose from his seat, and wrapping himself in an old grey surtout, walked around his camp. He paused by a camp-fire which was near the outer edge of his advanced lines. Around the dim embers were stretched several men, and at a little distance at the root of an old tree, lay one by himself. As the general approached the fire, he asked the solitary sentinel, who hailed him, if Captain Walker was near.

The figure which was reclining near the tree, at once arose and advanced. It was Walker.

"I am here, general, not asleep, though resting, after to-day's ride!"

"It is well for you to rest, sir, you will need all your strength to-morrow—but I have sought you to ask about our spy. He should have been here before now—I fear some casualty has befallen him! You are sure of his faith?"

"Yes, sir, as sure of him as I am of myself. If he is not killed he will be here soon, but you gave him a long and hard rout!"

"True, but he has been gone nearly two months, he must have heard of the death of Cross, and Thornton's capture ere this, and such news would hasten his return!"

"If he is alive he will be with us before another blow is struck, perhaps by morning!" replied Walker.

"I hope he will, for now that the war is commenced, I am determined to push it, aye to force a peace. The only way to make a victory valuable is to improve upon it—to push ahead. If a woodman in clearing up a piece of ground simply cuts down the trees, they are more in his way than ever. He must burn them up, as well as cut them down. So with us; we must not only whip the enemy, but we must disperse or destroy him?"

"I don't know much about the theory or rules of war, general," answered Walker, "but I'm willing to learn. I'm like the tailor's good apprentice

—you cut out the clothes and I'll sew em'up! No offence of course to your name sir!"

The general laughed; and said : "It would be hard to make me offended with so good an apprentice as you have proved yourself within the past ten days—in fact, I think it were no more than justice to dub you a journeyman !"

" I thank you, general—I'll try and do honour to the profession to-morrow, for you can hear by the drums and bugles on the road, ahead, that the bloody yellow-skins are getting ready for another skrimmage !"

ROUGH AND READY AT THE DEATH-BED OF RINGGOLD.—PAGE 18.

" Yes—and if they have stopped at the dry ravine a few miles up the road, they will bother us some !"

" Not much, general. A little of the bayonet and broadsword, will start them as it did to-day, and then we'll have more use for the spur than anything else.'

" You must not think too lightly of them. Some of their corps fought well to. and their batteries were well served !"

We mustn't let them use their batteries, sir. Leave them to Charley May's ons, and my mounted rangers, and see how long they'll hold their guns !"

No. 3.

"You shall have a chance at them, if they stand!" said the general, smiling, and then he turned away.

His next steps were to the temporary tent where rested poor Ringgold. By his side knelt Ridgley, his gallant friend and subaltern, who had so long been assisting him in drilling and forming his mounted artillery corps. Tears were coursing down his sun-bronzed cheeks—he knew that his commander and friend must die. May was there—the Murat of our army, with his jetty beard and flowing hair; and others as brave and true, were also near, but all fell back as their beloved general approached.

The eye of the wounded man brightened, as he saw who it was that knelt down on the ground where he lay and took his cold hand. The general could not speak —his heart was full—he saw that he must lose his most valuable officer. Let it be said as no disparagement to the rest of that brave band ; but beside the general himself, that army could better have spared any two of its officers, than one Ringgold.

"General, I have done my duty—have lived a soldier's life—I have met a soldier's fate !" said the wounded man, faintly.

The general's eyes filled, his lips trembled as if he would speak, but he could not. Pressing warmly the cold hand of the wounded officer, he arose and hastily passed from a scene which was far more terrible to him than the mad havoc of battle— the death-bed of a friend.

It was morning once more. The troops were up at the first tap of the reveille drum, and everything was ready for the renewal of their march. The spies had given the position of the enemy, and as it was known that another scene of carnage was at hand, and though they knew that the foe was far more numerous than they, still the Spartan band formed calmly into column and line, and advanced as steadily as if they were on parade. They were not long in finding the enemy. The general's order of battle on that day was simple; his directions few but strong. Keeping his artillery in the wood where it could be used, and flanking it with his infantry, he had advanced upon the foe ; his few mounted men, under May and Walker, kept in reserve near himself, ready to act when their time came. "The ball" opened, and then not long had May and Walker to wait. When the enemy's battery came into full play, then Taylor rose in his stirrups, and pointing towards it with his field glass—cried to Captain May :

"Your time has come sir, there is the enemy's battery, take it, nolens volens !"

Then did the gallant dragoons shout, in their mad glee, as their dark browed leader rose in his stirrups, and pointing with his bright sabre toward the foe, shouted:

"Forward men! follow !" And they did follow—on, on with bloody spurs, bright steel flashing in their hands, and brighter eyes flashing in their heads, they rode ; soon they were beside the gallant Ridgely's battery, and as he cried :

"Stop one moment, Charley, till I draw the fire off the battery !"

They reined into his right, then after he fired and received in return the fire of the enemy, again they dashed on to their leader's shout of—"Forward ! boys, forward !" and the next moment they were upon the foe, though met by a deadly fire which strewed near one half upon the plain. On, on like the tempest through the grain-field they swept, and the enemy reeled before the shock. Back once more they wheeled along the same gory path, and the battery was taken. The noble La Vega was a prisoner to us, but our Inge—"Fred Inge," the beloved of his corps and all the army, was dead; and many a bold dragoon lay cold in that bloody trench. Walker and his rangers, though they shared not in this charge, were in as perilous affray in another part of the field, and at this moment came up to join May, who had already delivered his distinguished prisoner to Colonel Twiggs, his immediate commander.

The enemy were not yet conquered, and were fighting desperately in detached parties through the chapparal. May and Walker was observing a body of l ... in their front at this time, who seemed preparing for a charge upon them ... suddenly they noticed a confusion in he enemy's ranks, and in a moment ...

they saw a soldier mounted on a magnificent white horse, dashing right through the ranks of the lancers, cutting right and left with a sword which was red with blood. Though he was dressed like a Mexican, his actions served to shew that he was not of them, but rather of their foes, and a fearful foe too; for as a mower lays a swath with his scythe, so did the strong horseman sweep a path before him. In a moment more he was free from them, and with a loud shout of joy, dashed down toward May and his little squadron. His horse was spotted over with blood—his appearance seemed like a demon of the battle field.

" By heavens, 'tis Brackett, my own Brackett!" cried Walker, as he struck spurs to his horse, and rode out to meet the spy.

" For God's sake, off with that sombrero and green jacket, Charley, or you'll be shot for a yellow skin!" he added, as he neared the horseman, who, was, indeed the spy, safely returned.

In a few moments they had returned to the ranks, and a hasty, and at that crisis very necessary, change was made in Brackett's dress.

" Now you look more like yourself, Charley!" cried Walker ; " but how you must have astonished the yellow skins when you dashed through them single-handed !"

" They did seem a little scared !" answered the spy ; " but I saw that I was late to the dinner, and thought I'd try and make a meal off the first grub that came in my way. Where's the general ?"

" God knows—I don't ; he's somewhere about, where fighting is going on, sitting cross-legged on his old white horse, laughing in his sleeve to see how our boys use up the yellow skins."

" I must find him—I've important news for him !"

" Which way did you come?"

' By the stockade—and its gallant commander, Major Brown is killed—but Hawkins is of the right breed, he'll hold it till all's blue again."

" What has detained you so long — the general was asking for you last night."

" It would take me all day to tell you ; but I must find him, and report my arrival !" The spy now galloped off across the battle-field in search of Taylor. He soon found him, for he was very conspicuous, as he sat carelessly upon his large white charger.

The eye of the General gleamed with pleasure, as he saw the ranger approach, and he hastily asked :

" Have you succeeded, sir ?'

" Perfectly, general !"

" Well, sir, I'm glad to hear it. The day is now our own, and this spree will soon be over. Come to me when all is quiet, and I will receive your report."

The ranger bowed low in his saddle, and was about turning to join in that which now was a pursuit and massacre, rather than a battle, when the general added :

" Take care of yourself, sir—I don't want to lose you at any time, but especially not till I have a report of your reconnoisance. Keep near my side."

This order Brackett, of course, obeyed ; but he chafed to hear the shouts of the distant pursuers, and not to be permitted to join the melee.

CHAPTER VI.

THE NIGHT AFTER RESACA DE LA PALMA'S BLOODY DAY.—THE RANGER'S REPORT.
THE ROAD TO MEXICO.—THE SCENE CHANGES TO BUENA VISTA.—THE ESCAPE
IS DISCOVERED.—ANGER OF ALFREDE—DIGNITY OF MAGDALENA.

IT was night, and the victorious American army was encamped upon the ensan-
guined field of Resaca de la Palma, a name which, though spoken in a foreign
tongue, thrills through every American heart, as warmly, too, as that of Saratoga
Yorktown, or Brandywine.

The surgeons were employed in alleviating, to the extent of their power, the
sufferings of the wounded. All were treated alike—both friend and foe, officer
and private. Though it was late, yet the noble patriot, Taylor, was passing another
sleepless night. Though he knew that the foe was thoroughly vanquished, yet he
knew that his own force was small, poorly provided for, and far from succour, and
it required all of his stern energy to meet the emergencies which surrounded him.
This night again he passed without a tent between him and the blue sky—his solitary camp-fire glimmered up from beneath a clump of trees, and by its light the
was examining a map of the country, taken on that day from the baggage of General
Arista. By his side was Brackett, pointing out the different fortified parts of the
road towards Mexico, and explaining, as he went along, the state of all parts of the
country.

"Can Monterey be taken easily?" asked the general.

"Not easily sir. It is a strong place. Three thousand good American artille-
rists and riflemen could hold it till doomsday; but it can be taken by Americans."

"You are right—perfectly right, sir. I could take the world if all Americans
turn out such men as have fought these two battles for me—but this Monterey.
is an important point. I must have it!"

"You will, sir, if you try!" was the enthusiastic reply of the young
ranger.

"How is the road from there to Saltillo?" asked the general.

"Good to the city, but narrow and rough beyond; it was there I met
with the mishap which caused my delay, and an adventure which would be
worth something in the hands of some poor devil of a novel writer!"

"Well, sir, let us hear it. I see that Captain Walker is on nettles to know
what it is."

"I was taken prisoner by a man who is my sworn and deadly foe—a colonel in
the lancers."

"By what plea did he dare to take you?—the war had not commenced
then!"

"He recognised me as one of the Texans who helped to whip him and his
comrades at San Antonio, some few years since, and knew that I had sworn to
kill him! He murdered—worse than murdered—my mother and sister."

"Did you kill him?" asked Walker, who had listened with breathless
anxiety.

"No; my horse stumbled as I fired, and I shot too low, killing his horse instead
of him; but I laid out a few of his men before they got me down!"

"You were wounded, then?" asked the general.

"Certainly, sir, or they never would have taken me. That alone has delayed
me!"

"But how did you escape?"

"That is the romance, sir! I was assisted by a young woman who was
near as pretty as an angel, and quite as good as one. I'm sure that in this case
she was my 'better angel,' for she certainly saved my life in two instances. In
the first, she prevented them from killing me outright when I was taken.

second, she effected my escape—supplied me with a fresh horse, arms, and all that I needed !"

"How did you escape, Charley, tell us that!" asked Walker, whose attention had been marked.

"Why, the lady got my sentinel drunk or asleep, I hardly know which, then unbarred my prison door, led me out through her father's garden, mounted me on the lancer colonel's own favorite horse, said 'God bless you;' and sent me off."

"Who was she?"

"The daughter of an old planter, who has a very pretty, romantic place, called Buena Vista, just beyond Saltillo, where the mountain gorges commence. It is a magnificent spot for a fight—hills on both sides—lots of ravines and tree-clumps !"

"You fell in love with the lady, of course, did you not?" asked Walker again.

"Why, no—not exactly. I do feel a little grateful for her kindness in getting me out of a bad scrape, and I'd like very much to see her again, but I'm not in love!"

General Taylor, who had been steadily gazing down upon the map, raised his head at this remark, and said, with a singular smile :

"You shall soon see her, sir, if she does not remove from that position. It lays directly in the road which I shall take to Mexico!"

This was a singular prophecy, but the reader knows how well it has been fulfilled.

* * * * *

We will now pass back to a scene which occurred in the house of Don Ignatio Valdez on the morning when the escape of the ranger was discovered.

Colonel Alfrede had risen early and passed to the room of the prisoner to order him to hold himself in readiness to be taken to Saltillo for trial. The sentinel was pacing to and fro before the door ; the door was barred as usual. The colonel ordered the sentinel to open it. The order was obeyed, but neither the astonished sentinel, nor the enraged colonel could discover the prisoner. The nest seemed all right, yet the bird had flown.

"What means this, sir ? What treachery is this? Where is your prisoner ?" demanded the colonel, in tones of thunder, of the trembling sentinel.

"I know not, senor. Antonio said that all was right when I relieved him, about an hour after midnight, and I will swear by all the saints in heaven, that he could not have escaped in my watch !"

"Where is Antonio—being him here ?" thundered the officer again.

In a moment the other guard was awakened from that which seemed a very deep slumber, and stood before his colonel.

"What has become of the prisoner ?" asked the latter.

"Is he not in the prison, senor ?"

"No, dog! where is he ? Who aided in his escape "

"As I love the Holy Cross, senor, I do not know ! He did not escape in my watch !"

"There is a lie between you two !" thundered Alfrede ; "and if I don't find out the truth, I'll have you both shot !"

"I have not moved one step from before this door since Antonio called me," said the first sentinel.

"And has no one approached the spot ?" asked the colonel.

"No one, as I live !" answered the soldier ; but while he spoke the keen eye of Alfrede was watching the countenance of the other, he saw it flush up as he asked this question, and at once mistrusted him.

"And you, Antonio—can you say the same? Beware, villain, how you deceive me, for I can read something in that blushing face of yours, which must and shall be told !"

"No one, senor, but the lady Magdalena, and she only brought the prisoner some wine and food."

"Did she not give you some, too ?"

"Yes, senor," said the trembling soldier, for he knew now that a lie would be worth his life.

"And did you sleep afterward ?"

"I could not help it, senor ; I never felt so sleepy before in my life."

"I believe you, you cursed fool. I see through all this now—she has played the traitress, and released him. By Heaven, but she shall rue it. Quickly saddle my horse and your own. One of you ride at full speed to the city, and let patrols take every road in pursuit. He must be taken. I will give five hundred pesos to the man who takes him, dead or alive, I care not which !"

The soldiers hastened to obey these orders, while the colonel returned in a fierce and angry mood to the sitting-room of Don Ignatio.

The latter marked his flashing eye and darkened brow as he entered, and asked what was the matter.

"Matter enough, senor ; matter enough, when my prisoner must not only be better loved than myself, but must be set free from my hands by your daughter !"

"What ! the prisoner loved—set free by Magdalena ?"

"Yes, Don Ignatio. Now, methinks, it is time to exert a little of the parental authority, of which you have been all along too sparing, when she leagues with the enemies of her countrymen."

"By my honour, I cannot believe this—I must hear it from her own lips !"

The old Castilian arose and stepping to a window which overlooked the court, bade a female servant call her young mistress and send her to him.

Meantime, with long and hasty strides, the enraged colonel was striding to and fro across the room, but he paused as he heard a step approaching through the passage way. It was one of the soldiers.

"Well, sir, what want you now ? Why are you not mounted ?"

"We have nothing to mount, senor," answered the man. "Your horse and saddle is gone—our saddles are where we left them ; but there is not a horse left to a stall."

"There, sir, see more of your daughter's honour and patriotism ! She has leagued herself with a horse thief, as well as——"

Alfrede paused in his bitter and sneering speech, as the maiden herself, dressed purely in white, stepped forth from an inner apartment.

"Well sir," cried she in tones contemptuous as his own had been, "why did you not finish your tirade of abuse. It well becomes one who could deliberately determine to murder a brave and defenceless foe, who had become his prisoner ; it well becomes such an one to abuse the fair fame of woman !"

"Donna Magdalena, did you not aid and connive at the prisoner's escape ?" asked he, in tones more mild and respectful than one would have thought he could assume. The father spoke not, but when he heard this question, he bent forward, expressing in look and attitude, his deep anxiety.

With a firm, but clear tone, while she gazed steadily in the eye of her questioner, she answered :—

"I assisted a wounded and helpless man, whom, to your cost, you know to be brave, to escape from the hands of a man devoid of honour, truth, or any of the qualities which make a man a soldier and a cavalier !"

As she thus spoke, he ground his teeth together through his lips, till the blood streamed down upon his jetty beard ; his eyes seemed like burning coals of fire ; his dark face grew purple with rage ; at first he laid his hand upon his sword, as if he meditated to attack her there upon her father's floor, then he turned to the father, who stood with his head upon his hand, and his face expressing the agony of his mind, and cried :—

"Now, Don Ignatio, you have heard—judge for yourself."

"Magdalena, what have you done ?" asked the father of his child, in tones so sad and subdued, that they called the tears to her eyes in one instant.

" My duty to a helpless fellow-creature, who was in imminent peril !" said she' calmly, but in a tone far different from that which had marked her address to Alfrede.

" Rather say, lady, that you preferred a new lover to the duty you owe your country !" said Alfrede, with a cold sneer ; but the lady paid no attention to the remark or its tone, but again spoke to her father :

" I could not bear that he, so young and so brave, should be deliberately taken to the city to be shot ! You heard Don Gustave plan his doom ; you know that dastardly as it would have been to execute a foe taken in arms, gallantly fighting, nothing but the step I have taken would have saved him from that fate !"

" Do you not love him, daughter ? Is the reason of your conduct not that which is given by Colonel Alfrede ?"

" It is not, my father. I do not love him,' said the beautiful girl, and her tone was so steady and so confident that her father could not, did not doubt the truth of her declaration.

Not so with the officer. With a frown upon his brow, and a curse upon his lips, he turned away, ordering his soldiers to find horses somewhere, and speedily bring them ; then, while his clenched hands and frowning brow alone told how deep and wild his anger was, he stepped closer to her side, and in a tone low, but deep, said :

" He has not escaped, lady ! no, by the bright heavens above—by the love I have borne for you, I will retake the miscreant, and you shall see him die !"

" He will not die till his mother and sister's fearful wrongs have been avenged !" answered she, in a tone as low and deep as his, a tone which did not reach the ear of her father.

Don Ignatio wondered as he saw Colonel Alfrede turn so suddenly pale, and utter with a curse :—

" Has he told you all ? Then. indeed, must he die. There is now no tampering !" But he knew not the cause of the paleness or remark. As he said this, without even the courtesy of a parting salute, the officer strode from the room.

The daughter kissed her father's care-worn brow, and retired to her own and her sister's apartment. The lovely twain shared the same room and the same bed. The room was that from which the latticed window opened to the road, the window through which she first had seen him. She had denied that she loved Charles Brackett, but, perchance, she knew not her own heart. Let the future tell.

CHAPTER VII.

THE SISTERS, AND A MOONLIGHT CONFERENCE.—THE SERENADE.—THE RANGER APPEARS.—A DECLARATION OF LOVE, AND AN UNINTENTIONAL CONFESSION.

WE do not intend to make our story a history of the Mexican war, and will only touch upon such scenes and incidents as are actually connected with the tale, therefore the reader must not be surprised when we pass entirely over the capture of Matamoras, and the onward progress of our victorious army to Monterey ; nor must he expect from us a description of the glorious battle, which placed "the flag of the free" upon the hoary battlements of that ancient city.

The thread of our story recommences after the capture of the latter place, at the time when our scouts were already dogging the footsteps of the retreating foe, who were hastening to join Santa Anna, at San Luis Potosi. Alfrede with his regiment of lancers, had participated in the shame and defeat of the Mexican army at

Monterey, and had retreated with his corps to Saltillo, which was already threatened by the intended advance of General Worth.

The spies of the Americans, and the Texan rangers, were already hovering about the latter place. Don Ignatio Valdez, still remained at Buena Vista, for he had learned that the Americans never harmed the peaceably disposed inhabitants of the soil, who did not join in the war, and he was rather too old to take the field against them, especially when he knew that in so doing he left his daughters without a protector.

After his return from Monterey, Colonel Alfrede had been more than usually attentive in his visits to Buena Vista, and so far as remarks or actions were to be judged, appeared to have forgotten or forgiven the agency of Donna Magdalena in the escape of the young ranger. But she knew full well that in this he was concealing the true feelings of his heart; that his was the most consummate hypocrisy. Her father, however, placed a far different construction upon his conduct, and gave Don Gustave credit for a nobleness and generosity, to which he surely, had no right. He even urged the suit of Don Gustave upon his daughter, and began to assume a tone of authority, which was as new to him as it was strange to her.

Colonel Alfrede supported this effort with a gentleness of manner, which won much upon the father's regard, and even the gentle Ximena began to chide her sister for not being more kind to one who appeared to love her so devotedly.

It was on a sweet moonlight evening, shortly after the capture of Monterey, that the two sisters sat at their window enjoying the pleasant air which came down from the mountains, for though it was in the winter time, the atmosphere was soft and balmy. The hour was late, or rather we should say early, for it was past midnight.

Months had passed since Charles Brackett had left Buena Vista, yet Donna Magdalena had not heard a word from or of him. Alfrede had studiously concealed the fact, that he had again narrowly escaped from his inveterate foe in the siege of Monterey; had carefully kept from her that he had even seen the ranger. Still that her thoughts were upon him, let the following conversation testify.

Magdalena while seated by the side of Ximena, frequently looked out upon the Saltillo road, as if she expected some one to come from thitherward, and even as she looked in that direction, a gentle, half-suppressed sigh, would rise from her heaving bosom.

"Why do you sigh, sister?" asked Ximena, "are you thinking of the young American?"

"I was thinking of him then, Ximena,—I often wonder whether he succeeded in regaining his countrymen in safety, and wonder if he be amongst those who are invading our country. I hope he is safe!"

"Sister, I fear me much that you love that young stranger!" said Ximena, gravely.

"No," responded the other, "I do not love him, yet I often feel as if it would please me to see him once more—at least to know that he is in safety!"

"Ah, my sister, such interest is very near akin to love. It is too strong a feeling for a virtuous and patriotic Mexican maiden to hold for one who belongs to the cruel nation which has invaded her plains, and drenched them with blood, who are even now revelling in the halls of our most beautiful city, and perchance may soon come to drive us from our happy home."

"Ah, sister, do not call my feeling love, or chide me now. I am sad enough already. My father is pressing the odious suit of Alfred upon me. Indeed he has given me no choice, and says that within two short weeks I must wed him—must, Ximena, must! 'Tis the first time he ever spoke so to me!"

"He acts for your welfare, my sister!" responded the gentle Ximena, but let us change the theme. Take your guitar, love, and sing for me. Sing my favourite, "La Ausencia."

The fair girl, with another sigh, raised her guitar to accede to her sister's request, and in a voice sad and sweet, sung a few lines.

She was about to continue with the second stanza of the song, when a rich manly voice beneath her window, took up the strain, and she heard the very words she was about to sing.

"Oh, Cielo! 'tis he—'tis the stranger!" cried the astonished Magdalena, as she let fall her guitar, and bent far out of the window, to look down in the shadow of the wall beneath. She saw a horse fastened beneath a tree at a short distance; she recognised the magnificent charger on which the stranger had rode away, the

ALFREDE SHOWS MAGDALENA THE DOCUMENTS.—SEE PAGE 30.

same which had belonged to Don Gustave. While yet she peered down into the dense shadow beneath her window, the singer stepped out into the moonlight, and she at once recognised the young ranger, dressed in a handsome uniform, and armed to the teeth. He had recovered his health, and the astonished girl fancied that she never had seen a more noble looking cavalier than he.

"Look, Ximena, 'tis he!" she cried, and the other sister, as she gazed out upon him, replied—

"He indeed is the same, and he is handsome—but, beware my sister of love, remember that he is our foe!"

No. 4.

"Oh, fear me not, Ximena ; but see he recognizes us—oh, I must see him and talk with him a moment. He is surrounded with dangers here. I must advise him to return to his friends !"

"No—oh, no !" cried the timid Ximena, "you surely will not seek an interview with him ?"

"I surely shall, sister ?" replied the beautiful girl, and as she spoke she waved a 'kerchief from the window. The ranger approached nearer, and she spoke in a low tone :

"Hist, Senor ! oh, you are very imprudent. Quickly remove your horse from sight ; meet me in the garden in the rear ; the gate shall be open."

The ranger turned to obey, and Magdalena hastily prepared to descend to th garden. Her sister in tears now besought her to remain.

"Oh, do not go, sister ! you know not the peril you encounter, both of reputation and discovery."

"The innocent have their own safe-guard, sister ; fear not for me. Await my return in quiet and peace ; I shall be gone but a moment. I only go to warn im of his danger."

"I shall await you in prayer," replied Ximena, as she saw Magdalena with flushed cheek, and trembling form, pass forth to meet the stranger.

When she arrived at the small gate which opened into the rear of her father's garden, Donna Magdalena found the ranger already there. As she opened it, he stepped within, and taking her fair hand within his own, raised it to his lips.

"Oh, senor !" she cried—"Why—why have you come here, when the whole country is in arms. It is scoured daily by Alfrede's lancers. A price is set upon your head. If you are taken, nothing can again save you !"

"Is my life an object of interest to you, lady ?" he asked.

She answered with but one word, yet the look which accompanied, and tone which uttered it, expressed more than a thousand words could have done. "Senor !" was all she said, but her look asked if she had not already proved that his life was dear to her.

"I beg your pardon, dear lady," he continued, "I was near here on duty, and I could not refrain from coming to try to see you once more !'

"But the danger, senor !"

"I am used to danger, lady—I have long been inured to it. I wished once more to see you, and express my thanks to you for saving my life, and to assure you that your last requests have been fulfilled !"

"The requests, senor ?"

"Yes, lady, those made when last we stood near this spot, when you bade me not to forget you, and if war occurred, to be kind to your countrymen. Those words, lady, and the remembrance of you, have saved more than one life in the mad rush of battle. The foe who cries to me for quarter, speaks in the name of Magdalena, and speaks not in vain !"

"Oh, I thank you, noble cavalier : I can almost forget that you are a foe !"

"Oh, quite forget, beautiful lady, for Americans are never foes to such as you. We oppose men like men ; we meet the helpless with kindness !"

"Oh, will it ever be so ; will not our beautiful valleys be laid waste, will not the helpless yet fly in terror before your conquering arms ?"

"When my countrymen forget mercy, and make war upon women and children, then will I desert them ; but that time will never come !"

"I pray God it may not !" said the fair girl, and then she added, "but you must fly from here—it soon will be day, and you will be fearfully exposed. Alfrede and his lancers are out early and late !"

"Aye, and they will always be too late for me !" responded the ranger, with a stern smile ; "they were early in leaving Monterey, though !"

"Did you see him there ?" asked the maiden.

"Ask him ! Nothing but the flag of capitulation saved him from my arm ; but we will meet again. He has had his warning !"

"The consummate hypocrite told me that he had never seen or heard of you since your escape," said Magdalena; but now I see through his drift—he attempts to conceal all his feelings, and is using every means to urge on his odious suit."

"Does he still persecute you?"

"Oh, senor, if to inflict his presence upon me daily; if to be ever pouring his fulsome compliments upon my loathing ear, is to persecute, then I am persecuted!"

"This shall not last long. Within a month our troops will occupy Saltillo. If he dare to resist, we will soon silence his persecution; if he flies, he will leave you far behind, for you and yours shall have safety and protection guaranteed to you here. Your father surely will remain?"

"Alas, senor, he this day swore upon his honour that I should wed the hated Alfrede, and gave me but two weeks to prepare for the sacrifice. Two short weeks only!"

"Ha! force to be employed, and that so soon?"

"Alas! senor, I speak that which is but too true!"

"Then force shall be met with force, lady. You nevr   wed him—never!"

"How can I be saved?"

"I shall be ever near you and ever on the watch. Fear not but that I will foil all plans that are attempted against your peace. Have you a servant in whom you can place all confidence?"

"I have one, senor; a faithful Indian boy, who would die for me!"

"Then if anything should occur which should cause you to require sudden assistance, send him with a single lock of your hair to a ranger camp which is in a wood near the forks of the road to Capellana. Bid him turn into the forest where it is most dense on the left, and sound this whistle. It will be answered speedily."

As the ranger said this, he took from his pocket a small silver whistle, which he presented to her, and she replied:

"I will accept it, senor, but never use it without my peril is imminent. I cannot forget that you are a foe to my country!"

"Oh, lady, do not say so: I would fain forget all things save that to you I owe my life— to you I have given my love!"

"Your love, senor? Oh, say not so!"

"Is my love so displeasing to you—am I so unfortunate as to love without hope?"

"Oh, senor, I know not what to say. You are the foe of my country!"

"But not yours! Oh, lady, forget that I am anything but your lover!"

"Senor, it is impossible—oh, what would my joy not be if this war had not occurred!" cried the maiden, and then as she felt that her unguarded expression had exposed more of her own feelings than she wished, she blushed and added. "Oh, leave me, senor, for the present at least. We may meet again, when this hateful war is past!"

"Oh, lady, one word which you have dropped, gives me hope. Say at least, though we may not meet soon, that my love is returned!"

"Senor, I dare not say all that I feel. You shall not be forgotten. I will never yield heart or hand to another!"

"I can ask no more than this, lady; you shall see me again; and, now, farewell!"

"Oh, be guarded, senor; dangers will ever attend you in this vicinity!"

"I will be careful, lady, for your sake!" responded the ranger. He bent his lips once more to her beautiful hand, the next moment he was gone.

For a moment the lady listened to his footsteps as he passed away, then she heard the rattling sound of his horse's hoofs as he galloped along the mountain base which ranged back to Saltillo. When all was still again, she burst into tears, and wept as if her very heart was running over.

Was it with grief? No, she loved for the first time, and knew that she was beloved. The fountain of true grief is one wherefrom few tears spring; it is the spring of joy, which, in a woman's heart, overruns its margin.

CHAPTER VII.

XIMENA AT PRAYER.—INTERVIEW BETWEEN MAGDALENA, HER FATHER, AND
ALFREDE.—THE DREADFUL ALTERNATIVE.—THE INDIAN MESSENGER.

WHEN Donna Magdalena returned to her chamber, she found her gentle sister
still bending on her knees by the window casement, with a golden crucifix in her
hand.

Oh, how beautiful that young girl looked, with her hands holding the sacred
symbol of her religion, and folded meekly across her heaving bosom! Her dark
eyes were looking calmly up towards the blue sky, as if already she saw that ther
was a place of rest prepared for her ; and her pure young lips were silently moving,
as if she communed with unseen spirits.

When she heard the step of her sister, she arose, and hastening to her side,
impressed upon her cheek a pure warm kiss of love and truth. When she saw the
trace of tears, she asked :

"What ails thee, my sister?" in tones, soft as the cooing of the wood-
dove.

"Oh, Ximena, I love, and love one of my country's foes !"

" I have long feared it, dear sister, but you must banish such feelings. Let pride
conquer them if nothing else !"

"Nothing can conquer love! Pride, all things must yield to feelings such as
mine. Long, long have I tried to control them, this single interview with him
proves how vainly !"

" But, dear sister, such love is hopeless. Our father has decided that you shall
marry Colonel Alfrede; besides, this war—"

" This war will not last for ever ; when it is over, he will come to honourably
claim me ; and for Alfrede, I would sooner die by my own hand than give th at l a d
to him whom I detest !",

Ximena saw that it was no use to combat feelings like these, and she went
sorrowing to her couch. Little did Magdalena sleep on that night ; yet when she
met her father in the morning, looking so bright and beautiful, and when he remarked upon it, she smiled and said,

" I am glad my looks please you, my father. These are kinder words than you
have been wont to use to your poor daughter lately !"

" Ah, child, if I have been harsh, it was for your own good—your happiness and
that of Ximena is all that I have to live for now !"

" But, my father, that which has been the plea of your severity, would be anything but happiness to me. I cannot love the man whom you would force me to
wed !"

" Say not force, Magdalena, rather say him who I implore you to wed !"

" You said I must wed him, my father, on yester-eve !"

" Oh, my daughter, if you knew all you would not think me severe. Much de-
pends upon this marriage, and I have set my very heart upon it."

"While I have set my very heart against it, dear father!" she said, playfully, and
then in a touching tone she added—"Can it not be delayed till this dreadful war
is over—now do delay it till then, and see if I do not become more reconciled to it
before then."

The father regarded his daughter sternly for a moment, but his look softened as
he gazed upon her beautiful and innocent face, so like that of his lost Seberina,
and he answered—

"I will see Don Gustave, my child, and I will try to gain his consent ; but he
has my promise, my sacred honour is pledged to him, and if he persists, then you
must——"

"Die, sir, die !" interrupted the passionate girl, "for know, that before will wed him with my present feelings, I will bury this dagger in my heart!" and as she spoke, she once more showed the pearly hilt of her bosom companion.

At this moment a servant announced that Don Gustave was riding toward the house, and the excited girl at once retired to her chamber.

In a few moments the colonel was announced.

Don Ignatio had not quite recovered his equanimity, but received his guest with his usual urbanity.

"The ladies are well, I hope?" said Don Gustave, as he seated himself.

"Quite well—that is, Ximena is, but Magdelena is a little indisposed this morning," said the father, hesitatingly.

"Nothing serious, I hope?" said Don Gustave, with great apparent anxiety of manner.

"No, senor—but I believe that the idea of this hasty marriage is injurious to her. Can it not be delayed till the close of the war?"

"Delayed, senor! Have I not wooed your daughter for years, have you not at last set the day which was to see me united to her, and now you ask for delay."

"Don Gustave, I have passed my word, but she insists upon delay, it is a painful thing for me to force this marraige."

"Is she more averse than usual to it?"

"Yes, this morning she threatened her own life, preferring death to a union with you."

"Will you send for her?—there is some mystery in this. I ask for a few words with her in your presence."

"I will have her called, Don Gustave," replied the father.

In a few moments the maiden made her appearance, and certainly she never had looked more beautiful than she did at that moment. Her face was flushed with a rich and rosy hue; her eyes were full and bright; her form seemed to dilate and swell into perfection with the air of queenly dignity, which seemed so natural to her.

"Lady, your father informs me that you wish our marriage delayed for a time," said the colonel, in a soft and pleasant tone.

"I do, sir, I wish it delayed for all time! You surely cannot wish my hand, if my heart goes not with it!"

"Has that heart been given to another?"

As the cunning officer asked this question, he intently gazed upon her countenance, as if he there could read the truth. Nor in this was he mistaken, for a deep flush overspread her fair face. She seemed to know this, and scorning all subterfuge, boldly answered—

"I have, sir, and who shall dare deny my right to do so."

"Is it my rival the traitor—the horse thief?" asked the colonel, sneeringly.

"Did you call him by those names when you saw him at Monterey, and turned from his conquering blade to seek safety by a timely retreat."

"Ha, lady! how knew you of this? The traitor must have met you; perchance he is even now lurking in the vicinity!"

"If so, then you had better keep well on your guard. Remember his mother. Remember the oath of revenge!"

The tone of the maiden in saying this was as cold and sneering as his own had been, and as she repeated the threat of the ranger, the villain quailed beneath the flashing glance of her dark eyes.

But he replied not to her remark, his brow grew darker as he drew a packet of papers from his breast, and handing them to her for perusal, remarked in a firm, but fiendish tone—

"I trifle no longer with you, lady. We must be wed! There, read and see if your father dare to refuse to urge the marriage on the appointed day."

One by one the maiden read each document, and then re-read their titles aloud.

"An agreement for my marriage in two weeks from yesterday—a mortgage upon my father's estate, and certificate of debt, to the amount of thirty thousand dollars—the last two to be null upon the accomplisment of my marriage !"

For a moment the maiden looked upon her father, but his face was hidden in his hands. With a wild energy she rushed to his feet, and as she held the papers before him, she cried—

"Are these true, my father ? Oh, are you thus in his power ?"

The father was dreadfully agitated, and seemed unable to answer. The colonel saved him this trouble, for in a colder tone than ever, he said—

"Look upon the seals and attests—each document is true and perfect. You see that there is a debt heavy enough to make you all peons for life. The fate of your father and sister is in your own hands. If you would see him, her, yourself, all slaves, then persist in your refusal to be mine."

The fearful truth seemed to strike home to the very heart of the poor girl. One only hope seemed left to her, and that was delay.

"Oh, if it must be so, let me have time to become reconciled to my lot !" she asked, in touching tones, "give me one year of freedom ?"

This stern answer came like ice to her soul.

"Lady, that agreement names two weeks, less one day. It must be fulfilled, or its forfeits shall be put in force."

"Heartless monster, you know the love I bore my father, else you would never have brought me to this alternative. Begone from my presence ; if I must be yours at the end of two weeks, at least let me be freed from your hideous attentions during that time."

"Lady, you shall have your own way in this, but at the hour appointed, I shall stand here before you with a priest at my side, ready to make you mine !"

As he said this, he took again the papers from her hand, and turning short upon his heel, strode heavily from the apartment. She shuddered when she heard his words, but she heard not his low mutterings as he left the room. He said—

"I go, lady fair, but you shall have a keen watch kept over your motions ! Nothing shall foil me now."

The father only raised his head after Don Gustave was gone, and then it was to look upon his daughter, with an expression of unutterable agony. She saw his look, and throwing herself into his arms, said, tenderly—

"Do not grieve, my father, your Magdalena blames you not ; for your sake she will be at least equal to her fate !"

Still the stern old man could not speak the feelings which choked his very heart : he simply sobbed, "My child !" then burst into a flood of tears.

*   *   *   *   *

It was late in the afternoon of that day before Donna Magdalena found nerself free from her attendance upon her father ; but the moment that she could do so, she hurried to a well-shaded arbour in the garden, and beckoning an Indian boy, of nineteen or twenty years of age, to her side, asked :

"Zalupah, do you love me enough to risk your life to serve me ?"

The young Indian, who was a delicate, but active formed youth, with eyes dark as a thunder cloud, and bright as the lightning within it, answered:

"Let mistress try Zalupah ; he will kill other men—he will kill himself for her !"

"I want no blood shed !" said the fair girl—"but I want you to take a long ride for me, and to deliver a message !"

"Zalupah is ready!" was the simple but all-expressive answer of the youth.

Donna Magdalena then described to him the location of the ranger camp, gave him the whistle, then severed a lock of her jetty hair, and bade him ride to the ranger's camp, and deliver it to him, whom the Indian well remembered as the wounded prisoner, and to tell him that the lady Magdalena was in peril, and wished him to meet her at midnight, on the second night from then, at the garden gate.

"Zalupah will go!" was all that the Indian said, as he left her side; yet Donna Magdalena knew that in his simple promise she could put more dependence than in all the oaths of more civilized men.

CHAPTER IX.

THE RANGER'S CAMP.—THE MANNER OF INVITING A MEXICAN COURIER TO STOP AND DELIVER.—THE MELANCHOLY TALE OF THE RANGER.—THE MESSENGER AND THE RAVEN TRESS OF HAIR.

WITHIN the dense shade of a thick forest near the Saltillo road, was the ranger's camp, the location of which he had described to Magdalena. Brackett, with a chosen band of twenty well-armed and well-mounted friends, had been sent thus in advance by General Taylor to watch all the motions of the enemy and make frequent reports; and he had chosen this general hiding place and rendezvous, because it was a convenient centre, and an excellent spot for concealment. It was so near the main road that the tramp of any heavy body of men on the march could easily be heard, and still sufficiently distant for the trivial sounds of their own carefully-kept camp not to be noticed.

Within a small cleared space in the bushes, which was entirely surrounded by the thick undergrowth, the party clustered around the dying embers of a little fire, which had been built in a hole dug in the ground, in the Indian way, when they are on a war-party. Their horses were tied also within the circle, with bags, in which perchance corn had been, hung like muzzles below their mouths. There were only eighteen men by the fire; two, therefore, were acting as sentinels, or were absent on duty.

The party were all conversing in a low tone, and a little apart from the main body sat Brackett, with one other only by his side, this person from his dress appearing to be also an officer.

He was, and we will introduce to the reader Lieut. Allen, a tall, finely-formed fair-haired, light-complexioned man, of about twenty-three or four years of age. At the moment of introduction, Allen had requested Brackett to relate to him that portion of his history which had caused him to join the "Bloody Rangers" of Texas. To this Brackett sadly acceded, and thus ran his story;

"I was, but a youngster at the time the Texans rose and declared themselves independent of Mexico, yet I well remember each era of the struggle. My father came into the country and settled upon the Austin grant just before that time, but he had been but a few days in the country when he died, leaving my mother, sister, and self with a small but comfortable property.

"I used daily to ride upon a little pony to my school, about five miles from where we dwelt, going in the early morning while the dew lay upon the grass and flowers, and returning when the sun went down behind the forest.

"We thought little of danger when the war began, for we lived in a retired and quiet spot in the country, and though we heard of many a fearful outrage at a distance, we little expected the enemy at our own door. One morning as I went forth to school, a bright, cloudless morning it was, one of those cool, clear days, when the birds sing louder than usual, and the flowers look brighter than ever ; my dear mother and beautiful sister kissed me tenderly as they ever did, and I was never happier in my life than when I rode away from the sweet little cottage which held them.

"I came back at night. The cottage was not there. Smoke arose from smouldering embers where it had stood. Oh, God, the agony of that moment ! I rushed to the side of the expiring fire—I called upon the names of my mother and my sister, yet no answer came. I ran madly through our little garden, and saw that the flowers had been trampled down—I reached my sister's favorite bower, the lattice of which I had myself made ; the vines which shaded it, I had planted. Before I reached it, I heard a feeble moan, this hastened my steps, and soon I saw —oh, God of Mercy ! such a sight as never—never will leave me. My mother lay dead upon the ground—my sister by her side, with just strength enough left to tell me the fearful fate which she and her wretched mother had endured, and to say that the hellish wrong had been perpetrated by an officer whom she described, and who had commanded a scouting party of lancers.

"She told me this—and then she died."

While the speaker related this dreadful story, the big drops of perspiration gathered upon his pale face ; the agony of a life-time's misery seemed to be centred in his soul. After a moment's pause, he went on :—

"I buried them—there on the ground where they died, there I buried them with my own hand. Then I knelt down over their corses, and swore by the holy love which I had borne for my mother ; by the almost idolatrous regard which I held for my sister ; by the noble blood which coursed through my veins ; by the Almighty God who made me—to be revenged ! to live for nothing but to avenge that fearful, nameless wrong which all the blood of Mexico could not wash away !"

"And that oath ?" asked Allen.

"Has not yet been fulfilled. I tracked and traced the fiendish officer till I i secured his name, and knew his person. Gustave Alfrede yet lives, but his time st coming !"

"Is he not a colonel of lancers ? Was he not at Monterey ?"

"He is and was. He is now quartered but a few miles from here. I am watching him as the falcon eyes his prey. I will make my swoop when I am sure to reach him !"

"By Heavens ! captain, in this, as in all things, I am doubly yours. Whenever the time comes let me aid in his punishment !"

"You shall, my friend. His time is near. He is now endeavouring to force a marriage with one that I love ; but he will find himself forestalled in all his aims."

The other was about to speak, when a low whistle was heard in the direction of the road. Both started, but they sat quietly down again as they saw that it was the absent two of the party. These rode up to the fire and dismounted.

One of them hurried to Brackett and handed several papers, saying :

"I just took these, sir, from a courier beyond Saltillo. He seemed in a hurry, but I sent him a request from my rifle to stop, which request he readily complied with, and then I rifled his pouch of these papers."

"They are valuable dispatches. General Taylor must have them immediately !" said Brackett, who had hastily looked them over while the other was speaking. "Take fresh horses," he added, "and ride at once to the camp with them !"

The man hastened to obey these orders. The excitement of the moment had produced a flush upon the ranger's face, which now faded away as he continued :

"After all this had passed, you need not ask why I joined the Rangers. When and how, I will tell you. The battle of San Jacinto was raging, the foes were ten to one of the Texans. Just at the moment when the latter were preparing for their last desperate charge upon the enemy, a boy—a mere boy, dashed into their lines, mounted on a small black Indian pony, which was white with foam. In the hand of the boy was a long hunting-knife—he had no other weapon. He arrived just at the moment when the gallant Houston had ordered the charge, and without touching bridle, or looking to the right or the left, that young boy led the way in the charge which won that day. On—on, amongst the flying foe, riding close to their sides, and driving his long knife home to the hilt in every Mexican whom he could reach, that boy rode. The Texans

BRACKETT AND DON IGNATIO MADE PRISONERS BY ALFREDE.

looked upon him as a supernatural being. Unharmed, unscathed, he dashed into the thickest of the fray, and his shrill cry—"revenge, revenge!" rung sharp and loud amongst them, yet no one knew who or what he was. He continued amongst the foremost in the chase, until not a foe could be found, and then sunk exhausted from his pony. The rangers who had seen his actions on that day, now picked him up, and bore him carefully to their camp. He soon recovered—his simple but dreadful tale was soon told, and from that hour he became one of them. He was at Mier—he was at Resaca—Monterey—that boy is now by your side!"

No. 5.

So much had Allen become excited by this strange and thrilling recital, that he could not give utterance to his feelings. He could only grasp his friend's hand and say—

"By Heaven! it is too much! I am your's for revenge, soul and body—and for ever!"

The ranger was on the point of replying, when again a low whistle was heard in the direction of the road; in the next moment a horseman was seen slowly pushing through the bushes, peering around as if he knew not exactly where he was searching for. Seeing that in his dress and appearance he was decidedly Mexican nearly half of the rangers sprang to their feet and raised their rifles. One moment more and the imprudent stranger would have met his death, but Brackett who thought that he had seen that dark face before, bade his men drop their pieces, and stepped out from the thicket where he could be seen.

Uttering a cry of pleasure when he saw him, the dark rider advanced to the ranger, holding out in his hand a long tress of jetty hair.

The face of Brackett turned pale as he saw it, and paler still when the Indian boy of Magdalena (for it was he,) said :

"Zalupah has found El Senor Americano! Mistress wants you to-morrow night at the garden—bad times for poor mistress!"

"What is the matter—is she in peril?" asked the ranger, trembling with anxiety.

"Zalupah was told to bring lock of hair to Senor Americano, and to tell him mistress wants him. Zalupah knows no more."

"Ride back, good boy, and tell the lady that I will be there, and be ware how you speak upon the road or elsewhere of having met me!"

"Zalupah understands," said the Indian, and in a moment his bridle was turned again toward the road.

When the ranger returned to his companion, he said,—

"Allen, I shall have to leave the camp in your charge again, to-morrow, I have duty to perform which requires my personal attendance."

"Has it anything to do with that lock of hair which you have wrapped so carelessly around your fingers?" asked the lieutenant.

"Yes, this is a sign that I had agreed upon with one who is persecuted by Gustave Alfrede, the murderer of my mother and sister. She needs my assistance, and I must hasten to give it."

"You surely will not go alone?"

"Yes, for I think she is in no immediate danger, else her messenger would have known of it. She probably wishes to inform me of some change in her prospects."

"It is dangerous for you to ride about alone, through a country filled with foes."

"I fear little for such danger while I've a good horse under me, and trusty weapons in my hand," replied the ranger.

"Where do you go on this mission?"

"Even that I cannot tell you now. I will return before the day after to-morrow," replied the ranger, "in the mean time keep up the surveillance of the road. All reports of importance must go at once to the general."

In a short time the young commander of the spies was in his saddle bending his way through the forest cautiously, his horse's head turned to the southward.

CHAPTER X.

THE TRYSTE IS KEPT, BUT A FEARFUL INTERRUPTION TAKES PLACE—THE RANGER
AGAIN A PRISONER—A NEW AND THRILLING DEVELOPEMENT—THE UNCLE AND
NEPHEW AND THE DOUBLE IMPRISONMENT—THE PLOT DEEPENS FAST.

IT was nearly midnight, the night when Donna Magdalena expected the
ranger to meet her at the garden gate. Zalupah had returned and told her that
he would be there, and now, with all the impatience of new-born love, and all the
anxiety which her situation had inspired, she was upon the spot, awaiting his
arrival. Her beating heart often misled her and caused her to think that she heard
his horse's galloping hoofs, but she had looked out many times in vain. The moon
had not arisen yet, had it she might, perhaps, have seen that her every motion was
watched, that her father's house was surrounded by spies, the chief of whom, Don
Gustave himself, was within a few few feet of her, so near that he could
hear the sighs that ever and anon broke from her heaving bosom. But she knew it
not.

At last the hour approached, and as she bent her ear eagerly forward, she
indeed heard the sound of a courser's feet borne upon the breeze, and in a
moment more he—her lover was by her side. Springing from his horse he
folded his arms around her beautiful form, and for the first time in life their lips
met in the warm touch of love. She did not turn from him with any cold
mock modesty; she did not try to hide the natural blush which came and went
like the flushes of sunset on a summer sky, upon her cheek; she returned both
the embrace and the salute with an ardour which, while it spoke her own feelings,
was like burning fire to the heart of him who stood crouching in the shade near
that gate, the cunning Alfrede. When he had threatened to watch her motions,
he had been in earnest, and if she had but heard his threat, she might have been
more careful. He had seen the Indian boy returning from the direction of the
mountains, with a horse evidently jaded by travel, and he at once felt suspicious
that something was concealed in this boy's unusual ride, especially as he knew the
boy to be a favourite with Magdalena. Hence the cause of the watch he had set
around her, and which he headed in person.

"You are kind, senor," said the blushing girl—as she withdrew herself from
the embrace of the young ranger, and led him to a seat close to the gate. "You
are very kind to come so promptly to me. I little thought, when you gave me the
whistle and bade me send for you in case of need, that the necessity was so near
at hand!"

"What is your danger, dear lady?"

"My father has given a written agreement to that detestable wretch, Alfrede,
that I shall marry him within less than two weeks. He has, I know not how, got
my father completely in his power, and now has sworn to force me to the dreadful
sacrifice!"

"Ha—ha, sworn did you say? I too have sworn, and the hour is drawing
nigh when my oath shall be fulfilled—but why do you start and tremble?"

"I thought I heard a sound as of some one breathing heavily near us!" responded the girl.

"It is only my horse panting—I rode rapidly, for I had to make a circuit to
avoid some new outposts, and I feared to be late to our tryste!" said the other, and
then added:—"Do you know the day when he proposes to attempt this marriage,
and where he will try to have the ceremony performed?"

"In two weeks less four days now, and he said that here to my father's house
he would bring the priest who should rivet the chain which would make me far,
far worse than a slave!"

"I will attend the wedding party, and I will not come alone! I will bring a goodly company to assist at the feast, men who will bring their own knives and forks and be their own carvers!"

"How, senor, do I understand you?"

"I will be here in time to forbid the banns, lady. He shall have a bride on that day, but it shall be such a bride as the villain deserves. Cold steel shall be all that he shall hug to his breast."

"Hark—I surely heard footsteps.—Oh, I fear that we are watched!" said the timid girl.

"Oh no, 'tis but the breeze rising as the moon comes up; you can see the limbs are beginning to move. None would be astir about your father's house at this hour."

"No, yet I know not why, but my heart is filled with an involuntary dread a kind of unconscious warning that an enemy is near, or danger is in our vicinity."

"You are too timid, dear one,—I apprehend no danger. And now let me ask one more question. When the villain Alfrede brings hither his priest, and I come to render the services of that priest useless to him, it would be cruel to cheat the reverend gentleman out of a job. Will you not promise then to be mine?"

"While our countries are at war? While we are foes by nationality? Oh, no, wait till the war is over, and then ——"

"Why do you hesitate?—say all!" cried the young ranger, trembling with anxious suspense.

"Then, if you still desire it, then will I be yours."

"It will not be long then, dear one, for soon a peace must ensue, and when the happy day arrives ——"

"You will not be alive to see it!" said a harsh but well-known voice at his side; and ere Brackett could move or lay his hand upon a weapon, his arms were pinioned from behind, and several stout men held and surrounded him.

"Oh, God, it is he—all is lost!" cried Magdalena, as she sprung still closer to his side, and clasped her arms around him.

"No, not lost yet," he quickly whispered; "the boy—let him fly to my band with the news."

The noise of the struggle had served to conceal that he had spoken to her, and when Don Gustave tore her from the side of the ranger, he knew not that already had one way of rescue been thought of and planned.

Her shriek, as she found herself and lover surrounded, had already aroused the inmates of her father's house, and soon they began to gather thickly into the garden, and in a few moments the voice of the old Don was heard, as he inquired what was the meaning of the alarm.

"I have only been interrupting a little love-chapter in which your virtuous daughter has borne a prominent part," said Alfrede, rudely pushing the pale girl towards her father.

The latter looked one moment at her, then at the prisoner, whom he recognised by the light of the torches which the domestics had brought out, and then in tones deep, and low, and sad, he asked,—

"Is this true, Magdalena? Have you held a midnight meeting with yon traitor, one who is an outlaw and a foe?"

"I have met yen noble cavalier, sir," replied the girl, her colour returning with her pride. "I met him at midnight, and have been watched over by the low spy and villain who disgraces in a thousand ways the uniform which he wears,—him to whom you would wed a Valdez, one of the proudest names of Spain!"

"A Valdez!" repeated Brackett, while a shade of astonishment seemed to cross his brow.

No one, however, heeded this remark, but the father responded to the daughter,—

"Girl, I little thought this of you! I have ever treated you kindly—I have been ever lenient to you, but now it is time to adopt more severe measures.— When you can disgrace the name of Valdez, by holding stolen interviews in the shadow of night with an unknown vagabond, you need not object to linking it with that of any cavalier who will do you the honour to look upon you!"

Again the prisoner repeated slowly the name of Valdez. There was something in it which seemed to touch his ear with singular effect.

"Don Ignatio, once more I shall have to make a temporary prison of your house —and this time I will see that no escape will take place!" said Alfrede.

"My house is at your service, Don Gustave, and that the prisoner may not again receive aid from the hands of my recreant daughter, she too shall learn the use of bolts and bars. She has said that she wished to be freed from your presence until the day of her marriage. She shall have her will, for until that day, she shall enjoy the solitude of a prison!"

"Let her room be one that looks out upon the road, if you please, Don Ignatio. There will be a court-martial held here on the morrow, and if I err not in my judgment, the next morning's sun will rise for the last time upon yon low-born spy!"

"Low-born, did he say? Is the name of Valdez that of one of the proudest of Spain's glorious families?" His tone was too low to be heard, yet when Brackett thus spoke, there seemed to be a deep meaning in his words, and while he gazed steadily upon the face of Don Ignatis, he murmured:

"It must be so—he is very like!"

While all this was going on, Magdalena had not been seen; she had bent her head down as if it were to conceal the feelings which overcame her, but while her head was bowed so low, she had torn, even up by the roots, a tress of her jetty hair, for she had no chance to sever it, and then having caught the eye of her faithful Zalupah, who stood among the crowd of servants, she had dropped it upon a bush where he could reach it unobserved, and then looked toward the gate. The faithful boy knew the meaning of the glance and sign, and at once divined the wishes of his mistress. While the others moved slowly on toward the house, he dropped behind, unobserved, and as soon as the garden was clear, took up the jetty token which the maiden had left upon the bush, then mounting the ranger's splendid horse, was in a few moments riding at full speed towards the camp of the latter, to bear the news of his arrest.

Don Ignatio was somewhat surprised when he heard the prisoner request a private interview with him, as they led him away to the same room which he had formerly occupied, but as the colonel had no fear of treason in him, and made no objections to the interview, he consented to it.

The door of the prison room was closed upon them. Then Brackett, whose arms were still pinioned, seated himself upon the settee, which had before time been his couch.

"Well, sir, what is the reason of your desire to see me alone; what can you have in common with the father of her whose affections you have inveigled, and whom you come to see by stealth, at midnight, like a common thief?"

"Senor," replied the ranger, "I asked not for this interview to hear reproaches —but to satisfy my curiosity upon one point."

"Well, sir, go on, let me know the point."

"You heard that cowardly colonel of lancers call me low-born!"

"Well sir, I know not that he was in error there."

"Did you not speak of the name and family of Valdez being ranked amongst the noblest of Spain's chivalry?"

"I did so speak, and I shall ever so maintain!"

"And yet I am low-born!" said the ranger in a tone of bitterness.

"What has your birth to do with the name of Valdez?" asked Don Ignatio, haughtily, and as he saw that the other hesitated in his answer, he added—"speak ir, and say that which you have to say speedily ; I have little time for dallying here !"

"Did you ever know Isabella Marin Valdez?" asked the ranger, and as he spoke he regarded Don Ignatio with a searching look. But it needed not any searching gaze to detect the surprise which came over the haughty Castilian when he heard that name.

"Know her ?" he cried ; "say where have you heard that name; oh ! what know you of her ?"

"She was my mother ; she is now an angel in heaven !"

"Your mother ? Oh, man—man ! prove that you speak the truth ; prove it, else I will curse you for bringing up her memory in vain to me. It is many years since I have seen her. Our father opposed her marriage with a foreigner; she eloped with him, and I have never seen my only and dearly loved sister since, nor had a trace of her. Prove that you are her son, or I will curse you for a base liar !"

"Look upon this ring," said the ranger, shewing a massive seal, graven with a coat of arms, "here is her family arms !"

The old Castilian looked upon the ring, then looked long and steadily upon the face of the ranger. For long minutes he regarded each feature, then, as if speaking to himself, said,—

"The ring might have been stolen—but her features never! Yes, you are, you must be my nephew. Your name—what is it?"

"Charles Brackett !"

"That was the name of her husband—yes, Brackett was the name ! she dead ?"

"Yes, father, mother, sister and all gone, and the last—oh! ask that fiend Gustave Alfrede how they died ?"

"He—has he ever seen them?"

"Go ask him, ask him how they died. He is their murderer, their worse than murderer?"

The young man bent low his head, and whispered but a few words to that old man, yet those words were like the blighting frost of death upon the hearer. His face blanched, his form quivered, his eyes seemed as if about to start from their sockets, his whole appearance changed. He gasped for breath ; then in tones husky with horror he groaned,—

"Oh ! holy God ; can all this be true ! Is he the fiend that would shame the very things of hell ! And he would wed my daughter. By the God of Justice, he shall die !"

The horrified Don Ignatio was about to rush forth from the apartment, when he was met at the door by the villain himself, who had again played the part of a spy and a listener.

With a cold sneer, the colonel said—

"You need not trouble yourself to change your quarters. Don Ignatio; you had best stay here to console your new-found nephew, for he is near the end of his days !"

"What mean you, base dog ? I surely am not a prisoner in my own house ?"

"You certainly are, and likely to be for some time, if you address me in terms so exceedingly flattering !"

"Sir, I demand my release instantly !"

"I regret that it is not convenient for me to accede to your request !" said the colonel, still in the same bitter and contemptuous tone.

The exasperated Castillian was about to rush upon the villain, who opposed his path, but a glance beyond him showed a line of sentinels with presented lances, and he only gasped :

"Oh, God ! my poor daughter—what will now become of her ?"

"She will be my bride within twenty-four hours. I shall give her that time for preparation, and no longer. The hour that makes her mine, ends the life of yon high-born braggart, for he shall witness the ceremony before he dies !"

"Oh, God, protect us all!" gasped the unhappy father, while with a fiendish laugh the demon-like Alfrede heavily closed the door upon the prisoners, and, after bidding his lancers guard it at the peril of their lives, he turned away to seek the unhappy Magdalena, and to inform her of his intentions.

"Twenty-four hours," murmured Brackett, after the door closed—"twenty-four hours—if the messenger has gone, there will yet be time, but oh, God, if his path should be intercepted, if he should not reach Allen, then indeed are we in this fiend's power !"

CHAPTER XI.

TURNING THE TABLES.—MAGDALENA MARRIED, BUT NOT TO ALFREDE.—AGAIN THE TABLES ARE TURNED.—REVERSE UPON REVERSE.—THE SEAL OF CAIN SEALED UPON A VILLAIN'S BROW.

THE second night had arrived—the night of doom for Magdalena and her unfortunate lover. It was a strange bridal party that. The father was present, but he stood a prisoner between two lancers; Brackett was there, but he] still was pinioned; the maiden alone stood free and unbound, and never, never, had she worn a look of greater dignity, a more beautiful appearance. Strange as it may seem, she was comparatively calm, though her eye ever and anon wandered with a quick, anxious glance towards the door.

Alfrede, too, looked often toward the door, and the reason could easily be told, for he stamped his spurred boot heavily upon the floor, and in tones which betokened his impatience, cried :

"Curses on the head of that laggard priest, why comes he not?"

The domestics of the house, with pale countenances, stood in a corner of the apartment, near the door, wondering what next was to happen, for, though devotedly attached to their master, they were completely overawed by the superior force of well-armed soldiers, who guarded the house.

Toward this group the eye of Magdalena turned, as she saw a slight bustle amongst them, and that eye brightened with joy as she saw a new addition to their number, and in him recognised her faithful Indian boy. A look of intelligence passed between them, the Indian in it signified that all was right; but the keen eye of Alfrede was already upon him, and darting into the cowering crowd of servants, he caught the slight form of the boy in his grasp, and dashing him on the floor, placed his sword's point at his throat, shouting,—

"Where have you been, you black dog? What treason have you and your mistress been hatching now? Speak, or by the God who made you, this moment is your last !"

The Indian neither moved nor spoke. The sword of the enraged officer was raised to strike the fatal blow, when at the instant he was nerving his arm for its descent, his weapon was dashed from his hand by the heroic Magdalena, who had snatched a weapon from a soldier who stood near her. At the same moment the two doors of the apartment were burst open, and Allen and his rangers with presented rifles filled the room. The lancers saw these dreaded weapons and in an instant dropped their arms. Alfrede alone would have resisted, but his weapon was gone, and in a moment he was pinioned, while Don Ignatio and Brackett were once more free.

At this moment the priest arrived, and now Magdalena, with all of the arch mockery of manner which she could assume, walked up to Alfred, and asked him if he was ready to have the ceremony proceed.

The discomfitted villain would not answer, but if his face was a picture of all that was working within his breast, hell itself would have been a paradise to it.

But it seemed now as if his cup was not full, for Don Ignatio, who had been conversing in a low tone with Brackett, turned to his daughter and asked,—

"Magdalena, do you love this cavalier?"

"I do, my father," answered the blushing girl.

"Wilt thou wed him? My consent is given, for he is thine equal in birth, he is thy cousin?"

"My cousin?" asked the bewildered maiden.

"Yes, my child; thy father's nephew—Charles Brackett, the son of my sister."

Pale turned the face of Gustave Alfrede as he heard these words, and paler still when Don Ignatio approached him, and hissed one word in his ear. It was but a word—"*remember!*" and yet it sounded like a death-knell unto him.

Again he heard it, louder still from the lips of Brackett, that fearful word—"*remember!*"

Oh, there is to the guilty something more terrible in memory, than in all other things. It gives a double terror, for it links the past with the present and the future.

At this moment the gentle Ximena appeared, having been informed by the domestics of the happy change which had ensued in her family's situation, and after her father had briefly explained to her and Magdalena the relationship of Brackett, he once more proposed that they should be united upon the spot, by the priest whom Alfrede had sent for.

To this no objections were made, and then, at the still, solemn hour of midnight, before all those witnesses, Charles Brackett was united to his beautiful cousin. While the ceremony was being performed, the firing of cannon was heard in the direction of Saltillo, and Allen hastily despatched a couple of his scouts to see what it meant. The ceremony had been over but a few moments, when these returned, and reported that the garrison of Saltillo was in full retreat along the road toward the house, thus shewing that the American force under Worth had arrived in the town.

For a moment only, Brackett paused to consider how he should act. The scouts reported that the enemy were several thousand strong; he knew that resistance would be useless; therefore he determined at once to retreat with his prisoners, leaving Don Ignatio and his family at home, for he knew that they, of course, would be safe, and he could rejoin them on the morrow. To this plan Don Ignatio gave his assent, and snatching a hasty kiss from his bride, Brackett, and Allen, with his rangers, left the house, taking with them Alfrede and his disarmed band of lancers. In a few moments all were in their saddle, and Brackett started with them up a ravine which, by a circuitous route, led to the rear of Saltillo. The moon had now arisen, and it was a beautiful sight to see those armed men file silently along, now in shadow then in light; now hidden in some little glen, then emerging over some little hillock, when horse and rider would lay their shadows upon the rocks beyond them. And it was a beautiful sight, but not a very romantic one to them, at least not a pleasant one, when they saw ahead of them, riding down the same ravine, a body of the enemy's lancers; and as they knew that, encumbered as they were, it would be impossible for them to break through this force, they determined to turn rein and seek another and a safer route.

This was done; but soon Brackett found that the danger in his rear was greater than that in front, for the main body of the retreating army occupied the road, and it was now impossible to avoid one or the other of them. He held a rapid consultation with Allen, as to how he should dispose of the prisoners. The advice of the latter, was to free all except Alfrede—to kill him upon the spot, then to cut their way through the lancers in their front. But all of this did not suit the too noble mind of the young ranger captain. His foe was in his power, but he could not murder even him in cold blood. "Oh, that I had but five minutes left to us on a fair field, I would let God prove the right!" he cried; "but I cannot kill even him without a weapon in his hands. I had intended to have tried him regularly, by a jury, and to have hung him for a murdering dog as he is; but I cannot slay even him in cold blood, when he is entirely in my power!"

The party had in this time come to a halt, and Alfrede, who was bound upon his horse, and rode between two of the rangers, cast uneasy glances round him, for he seemed to know that the conference between Allen and Brackett concerned him, especially as Allen had used several pantomimic actions, such as laying his hand upon the hilt of his heavy bowie knife, pointing to his throat, and so forth; and the villian feared that the ranger would act as he would have done, had the tables been turned and they in his power.

Brackett, at last, with a singular smile, said to Allen—

No. 6.

"I have formed my plan, George, we cannot afford to be hampered with prisoners!" Then riding to the centre, were they where sitting, bound upon their horses without arms, he bade his men turn the prisoners' reins to the south, and, speaking to them in their own tongue, he bade them ride to the army and thank their stars that he did not slay them on the spot. But when he reached the side of the black-hearted Alfrede, his look was fearfully dark and ominous. The lancer officer turned pale as death, when he saw the ranger deliberately draw his large bowie knife from its sheath, and as the latter approached him, he shuddered, and gasped—

"For the love of God, sir, do not murder me!"

He trembled more than ever, as he saw the unrelenting expression of the ranger's face, and when he saw that bright, broad-bladed knife raised in the air, he closed his eyes, for he thought that his time had come.

The next moment he felt its keen edge, as Brackett, with a quick and skilful hand, cut a gash into the bone, down the centre of his forehead, from the hair to the spot where his dark eyebrows met, and then he thought he was to suffer a most painful death, and he again gasped—

"If I must die, oh, kill me outright, do not torture me!"

But the ranger spoke not a single word to him, he again raised the blade, now darkened at its edge with blood, and with the same skilful touch, drew a gash horizontal to the other, thus making upon his forehead a large red cross.

"Now, thou dog of hell, I've marked you, so that when next we meet, be it in the smoke-cloud of battle, or in the glimmering light of a starry night, I may know you; and when next we meet, remember that I will fulfil the oath of revenge! Think not to escape me—you are marked, and if I should die, every friend I have on earth would dog you by the sign of the bloody cross upon your brow!"

With a groan of mingled pain and rage, and fear, the marked villain heard these words, then saw Brackett turn his horse's head to the south, and drive his pointed knife deep into the tender flank of the animal. With maddened speed the horse bounded off toward the Mexican army, bearing his helpless rider along with him.

When this was done the ranger quickly formed his little band into a solid phalanx, himself taking the head, and Allen, much against his will, but in obedience to orders, closing up the rear.

"You must ride and fight for your lives now, men. Keep close, support each other, and follow me!" said Brackett in a low tone.

For a moment there was a tightening of each man's grasp upon his rein, a movement to fix his seat firmer in the saddle; then again their commander's low tone was heard:

"Spurs will avail you more than your blades. Draw only a revolver, press close upon me, and drive through their ranks! It is your only chance, we are but twenty, they at least a thousand!"

Then, as the moon's rays glanced down upon the bright lance-heads, and a forest of waving pennons, which were now close upon them, their brave leader shouted:

"Forward!"

With one wild cheer, they sunk their rowels deep into their horses' flanks, then on, on they dashed like one huge black wave rolling up singly and alone over a thousand lesser breakers on some rugged shore. One moment more and they were upon their foe, and then their leader shouted again: "Fire—give them lead"

and the little band poured in a rapid volley from their unerring revolvers. Had the foe met this charge boldly, like men, it would have been much easier for the heroic little band to have cut its way through them; but they reeled back in confusion and fear, and the foremost of them attempted to fly. This act threw their whole column into a medley mass, and made it impossible for the rangers to ride through them, though they succeeded in penetrating to some distance, but this in the narrow ravine, made their situation still worse.

"To your knives, boys,—give them steel now!" shouted their captain, and then the fearful bowie knife began its murderous work. But the Mexicans were not idle now, for they saw how few were their enemies in number, and they fought for very shame. The rangers now began to drop one by one, by the side of their gallant leader, yet for every one of them fell many of the foe.

The commander of the lancers, a noble-looking, grey-headed man in the uniform of a general, now shouted to Brackett, begging him to yield, promising, on his honour, to treat him with the courtesies of a prisoner of war.

Brackett looked around him—more than half his men were gone, the rest were fighting gallantly; but he knew it was in vain that they struggled against such fearful weight of numbers, and he asked to whom he must surrender, if he yielded.

"To General Vasquez, of the regular army!" was the reply of the grey-headed officer whom we have above alluded to. Brackett knew that this officer, by reputation, was one of the most gallant and brave in the Mexican army; he also knew that gallantry and honour in a soldier, are inseparable; therefore, to save the lives of his gallant comrades, he surrendered his sword to Vasquez.

The rangers were then surrounded by a strong guard, and their horses' heads turned to the southward. The Mexicans were on the retreat to San Luis Potosi, where Santa Anna was collecting an overwhelming force, with which he had pledged himself to the "magnanimous Mexican nation," to drive "the perfidious Yankees" beyond their utmost borders.

CHAPTER XII.

GLORY OF THE AMERICAN SOLDIER.—THE LOVE OF WOMAN,—THE DISGUISE.—THE INTERVIEW BETWEEN THE FOES AGAIN.—THE THREAT.—DONNA MAGDALENA IN DANGER.

It was morning. The "flag of the free" waved on the battlements of Saltillo. Not an armed Mexican was to be seen in its streets, all was quiet and orderly, more so than perchance it ever had been before. But few of the houses were closed, the citizens seemed perfectly at their ease as they opened their shop doors to trade with the new comers, or perambulated the streets to gaze upon them at their different posts. Saltillo had been taken—bloodlessly, noiselessly, and now not a sound of rejoicing over an humbled foe was heard from the lips of the victors; they were quiet, orderly, as well behaved as they would have been in their own cities.

Oh noble—noble has been the conduct of the American victors in this war. Let their conduct at Monterey be held up as an example to a whole world. For weary days they fought before that rich city—hundreds of their best and bravest fell before their eyes, yet when the victory was gained and a rich city lay open before them, when the temptations of uncounted wealth came and knocked at their hearts, though they were suffering for clothes and food, not one of all that noble little army was known to commit a single outrage upon the vanquished foe, even though there were men there whose relatives had been butchered in the "Alamo," or whose families had been robbed and murdered on the gory plains of Texas.

Oh, let such conduct be written in letters of gold on the fairest pages of the country's history, that every American heart in ages yet to come may proudly point to the starriest spot in all its glorious escutcheon.

It was morning, and not a Mexican soldier was in sight from the case at Buena Vista.

Yet there was mourning and sorrow in that house, for they had heard the firing on he night before, immediately after the departure of Brackett, and knew by this that he had been intercepted.

Sleep came not to the eyes of the newly wedded bride on that night, and soon as the dawn came to light up the east, the servants were dispatched up the ravine to see if they could gather news of the rangers.

Soon they returned, bearing with them one of the rangers, whom they found still alive upon the battle-field. The rest who had fallen were all dead, but they lay amid a heap of fallen foes, enough in number to have hidden them from sight.

The one whom the servants brought in was dying, yet he lived long enough to tell the fate of his comrades, and to say what had become of Alfrede and his lancers, and to tell how the latter had been marked for vengeance.

Pale turned the cheek of poor Magdalena when she learned that her husband was a prisoner in the hands of her countrymen, and that Alfrede was again free, and had now a double incentive to revenge.

The fears of Don Ignatio, too, were excited, and he determined at once to communicate with General Worth at Saltillo, and inform him of the fate of the rangers, in order if possible to have them exchanged or rescued in some way.

Magdalena, too, formed a determination, bold as it was sudden, and one that showed well what a true woman's heart is capable of when she loves and her beloved is in danger. To let the reader into the secret of this, we must give them the substance of a scene which occurred in the favourite arbour of Donna Magdalena in the garden.

She had gone thither, taking with her Zalupah, the faithful Indian boy, whom the reader already knows.

When they were secure from observation, she said :

"Zalupah, do you love your new master the noble cavalier to whom I was married last night ?"

"Zalupah loves all who love his mistress !" replied the boy.

"Your new master is a prisoner!"

"Zalupah is sorry ; he will go help to get him away !"

"You cannot go alone ; he has many guards !"

"Zalupah can crawl like snake in the grass, get close to guard, stab 'em, and let his new master out of prison!"

"If they catch you they will kill you !"

"Can't die but once, Zalupah isn't afraid to die. His father died long time ago!"

"But you will need help. I will go with you, Zalupah."

The boy's large black eyes dilated with wonder and astonishment as he heard this. Shaking his head, he said :

"Mistress go? Oh no! feet too small, road too long. Bad man see her, bad man treat her cruel. Colonel Alfrede not dead yet—Zalupah will kill him when he catch him, but mistress must stay here. Zalupah will go alone!"

"No—I shall go with you!" replied the maiden bride firmly—"You must get me a dress like your own, Zalupah; I shall stain my face and hands dark, and dress like you. Nobody will know me then!"

"Foot and hand too small—shape too pretty !" said the Indian, and again he shook his head.

In a tone now so firm that he dared not disobey it, however so much he wished, Magdalena bade him provide her with a dress like his own, with good weapons, and to have two of her father's best horses saddled and ready for the journey as soon as darkness came over the sky. She had determined to follow her lover and to effect his rescue, or to perish by his side.

We will now follow the fortunes of the unfortunate ranger and his companions, who were retreating with the Mexican army towards San Luis Potosi.

They halted not until they had reached Guadalupo on the next evening, for they thought that the whole American army was in pursuit.

It was not until this halt took place that Colonel Alfrede, who, with a patch over his forehead to conceal his disfigurement, had ridden on in moody silence, at the head of his corps, learned of the capture of Brackett and his comrades, for his wounded and frightened horse had borne him far beyond the sound of pistols ere the combat began, which had resulted in their capture.

Our pen cannot paint the fiendish joy which filled his breast when he heard that Brackett was captured, and he at once flew to General Vazquez, and demanded that the prisoner should be turned over to him.

"On what grounds do you claim him,—what right have you to him?" asked the general, sternly.

"He was an escaped prisoner from me—I had captured him but the evening before?" replied the colonel, who in his eagerness betrayed his enmity.

"Then in losing possession of him, you lost all right to him!" replied the old general.

"He is a spy and a traitor! I demand that he be tried and treated as such!" cried the colonel, now excited beyond the bounds of prudence.

"He surrendered to me as a prisoner of war, after gallantly fighting till half of his men were slain, and as a prisoner of war, as a brave and honourable man shall he be treated till he is exchanged for some officer of our own of his rank, who meets with a fortune similar to his!"

"Exchanged!—What, shall he escape me! Sir, he is my enemy. Look here!" and the enraged officer tore the patch from off his forehead—"look at this, sir! This is his mark,—shall a man live who dares to treat me so? Think you that I shall let him escape my vengeance? No—by the high God of heaven! *No!*"

"Sir, if you threaten thus the life of my prisoner, perchance you may find yourself placed beyond the power of harming him! Use but one more tone or gesture so disrespectful as your last, and I place you under arrest!"

The colonel saw that he had gone too far, and in a lowered tone, said:

"I beg your pardon, General Vasquez, but he is an ancient enemy of mine, and that, with this last damning insult, is enough to drive me beyond all bounds."

"Have you never given him cause for enmity, sir; have you never injured him?" asked the general, still speaking with unbending sternness.

The colonel's face flushed and darkened as this question was asked, and the general, noticing this, turned to an orderly near him and bade him bring Capt Brackett before him! The colonel now endeavoured to make an excuse to leave the spot, but his countenance had paled too suddenly to allay any of the suspicions of the cunning old general, and in a tone more severe than before, he ordered him to remain until the prisoner had confronted him.

In a moment more the sworn foes stood face to face.

When General Vasquez asked of Brackett the cause of this terrible enmity, and while he listened to the harrowing tale of wrong, frequent and loud were his bitter tones of condemnation; and when Brackett related the scene where he had affixed the Cain-like mark upon him, the honest-hearted old general cried:

"'Tis well that he is thus marked! It and its cause shall be known througout the army, and no worse punishment can be inflicted than that which draws down upon him hissings and the universal scorn of the whole army: the contempt of all honourable men!"

Then turning to the colonel, whose face was livid with mortification and rage, he added, in cold and bitter tones:

"Go, thou disgrace to a soldier's name; go, and if I ever find you near my quarters again, you shall be whipt from their vicinity by the scullions of my camp!"

The colonel attempted to speak, but the choleric old general burst out with a fresh volley of invectives:

"Begone, thou Cain; begone from my sight, I hope that soon I shall have a chance to exchange or free my gallant prisoner; for I sigh for the time when I may hear that he has met thee once more upon a fair field!"

The colonel, now completely discomfitted, turned away, his face presenting a picture which would well have suited one who wished to make a painting of a devil in hell.

"I can reach you yet!" he hissed, in tones that, from the fearful import of the threat which followed, went like ice to the heart of Brackett, who alone heard them—"I can reach you yet, my revenge shall be deeper that it is through another, and doubly shall it fall upon you, for *she* shall now be mine!"

These words were indeed fearful to the ranger. He knew that his virgin bride and her family were without a protector now; he knew the fiendish feelings and wild lust which filled the heart of his enemy, and he trembled for those whom he could not now protect.

He would have given worlds now to have recalled the act of mercy, the feeling which induced him to spare the villain when he had him in his power. These feelings were only the more increased when, to his utter agony of heart, a short time afterwards, he saw the fiend ride off to the northward with a small body of lancers in his train, and his tortured mind was left to paint a thousand horrors. He saw his helpless bride shrieking in the lustful villain's arms, shrieking in vain for aid from others; for mercy from him! Oh, God! who—who can paint the feelings of a husband's heart in such a situation. It is far—far beyond our feeble powers.

CHAPTER XIII.

NEVER did mortal suffer greater agony of mind than the unhappy Brackett in his prison at San Luis Potosi. His only friend amongst the enemy, General Vasquez, was now too intently engaged in drilling his brigade and preparing for the next contest, to visit him. Amongst the groups of officers whom he could see upon the plaza which fronted his prison grates, he never could see the hated form of Alfrede, and his mind was left to imagine all kinds of horrible possibilities.

The few days he had been confined there had been to him as months. If he would have given his parole not to attempt to escape he would have been allowed the freedom of the city; but this he would not do, for he ever hoped for some opportunity to escape. He was confined separately from the rest of his band: therefore had nothing to cheer his mind up, or to drive away the fearful visions which continually arose before him.

We will now take the opportunity of chasing Colonel Alfrede on his mission of revenge.

True to his threat and purpose, he had bent his course back to Buena Vista; but when he arrived there he found that not only Magdalena was absent, but also Don Ignatio and Ximena. From some of the frightened domestics he gained the information that Donna Magdalena was missing, her father and sister knew not where, and that the latter had fled to the city and placed themselves under the protection of the Americans. His first act was to set fire to the building, and soon all, save its massive walls of stone, was destroyed. With a fiendish smile of exultation, he watched this scene of devastation; but when he saw that troops were despatched from the city to reconnoitre it and its cause, he hastily withdrew with his forces.

On learning that Donna Magdalena was not with her father and sister, and had suddenly disappeared, he at once conjectured whither she had gone, and at once retraced his course to San Luis Potosi : not, however, proceeding far in his own character, but assuming a disguise which enabled him to conceal the scar which not only disfigured, but marked him so singularly. This was the cowl and gown of a Dominican priest. He gave his lancers orders to return to their camp, and, under the security of his disguise, pursued his journey alone. Every desire of his heart, every thought of his mind, every energy of his soul and body was bent upon one object, that object—revenge. He was now determined to forego all things else ; and his revenge embraced a wish for the death of Brackett and the possession and ruin of poor Magdalena.

The disappearance of the latter caused unutterable misery to Don Ignatio and Ximena ; for they knew not whether she had fallen into the terrible hands of Alfrede, or had taken the dangerous resolution to follow her husband and to share his perils and captivity. When they found that their dwelling was destroyed by Don Gustave, which they learned from the frightened domestics, they for the first time learned that the villain was ignorant as themselves of the whereabouts of Magdalena, and in this they had some comfort, though they feared much that she yet would fall into his hands ; for now they had no doubt but that she had sought her husband in the Mexican camp.

The reader, especially if that reader be a descendant on the side of Eve, undoubtedly has a great curiosity to know where and how the lady is situated. We will accommodate him or her, as the case may be.

In the suburbs of the town of San Luis, are a vast number of little mudcottages. These are mostly inhabited by peons or slaves, or by the lower classes of society. In one of them, a few days after the destruction of the house at Buena Vista, were two persons. Both were nearly of a size, both dressed similarly, both nearly of the same hue, being full as dark as a New Orleans quadroon, or a Seminole Indian ; yet there was a vast difference in the points of the two. The eyes of both were large and jetty black ; yet the eyes of one were fierce, and sharp, and flashing, as are those of a serpent ; the eyes of the other were soft dewy and mournful in expression. The hands and feet of one were small and perfect ; while those of the other were coarse and clumsy. Both were habited in the usual costume of the peons of the country. The reader, of course, recognises Magdalena and her faithful Indian.

The latter had just come into the hut, and was speaking to his mistress.

"So you saw him, Zalupah ?" asked the latter.

"Yes, mistress. I sold soldier some aquadiente, and when I took him the bottle I saw my new master !"

"How did he look? Was he sad and sick ?"

"He looked like the lazy cloud in summer—white. He looked as if his rthea was dry, and no blood for his face."

"Did he see you ?"

"He didn't know me—Indians all look same—he not know Zalupah when he do see him !"

"He would know me, and yet I dare not go near him in the day time, for fear of discovery !" sighed the poor girl ; "and yet I must see him. How can you get him out?"

"Creep up to guard in night time—stab him in the throat, so can't make noise, then break open door."

"It is a fearful risk, yet something must be done, and that soon !" sighed she sadly.

The faithful Indian knelt by her feet, and, looking up in her face with his usual expression of devotion and respect, said :

"Zalupah try to-morrow night—dark come soon, no moon now !"

"God bless thee, my faithful boy ! If you succeed, you shall have your freedom and a rich reward !" said the lady, while her eyes filled with grateful tears.

PUBLISHER'S NOTE

pp.49-54 are missing.

"Zalupah don't want to be free—he never want to leave his mistress !" said the boy, earnestly.

When this conversation was going on in the hut, a far different scene was enacted in another hut near there, but the motives and feelings of the party were far different.

A man in the habit of a priest was conversing with another dressed as an officer in the Mexican army. The latter was a captain in the brigade of General Vasquez.

"It will be your guard-night, to-morrow evening, will it not, Captain Morelo?" asked the one who was clothed as a priest. We forgot to note above that his cowl was drawn almost entirely over his face.

"I am officer of the night for to-morrow eve !" answered him whom the other addressed as Captain Morelo.

"And you are willing, on certain conditions, to give orders to admit me to the American prisoner's room—Brackett's I mean."

"On certain conditions, Don Gustave !" replied the other.

"And those conditions are——"

"That you first give me a sufficient sum to fit myself out completely for the war with a fine horse, arms, and all equipments; second, that you have me advanced to a majority in your own regiment; third, that you give me means to bribe my sentinel not to divulge my orders; fourth that in killing him, you leave the dagger in his own hands, as if he had committed suicide !"

"Well, sir, you have quite a string of them, but they are all such as are within my power; therefore I accept them all, and at the mid-watch, on to-morrow night, I shall be upon the spot, robed as I now am. and then *he* shall *die !*"

CHAPTER XIV.

THE ASSASSIN FOILED THE ESCAPE.— MAGDALENA IN THE POWER OF HER ANCIENT
ENEMY.—DEATH TO ZALUPAH.—RESCUE OF THE VIRGIN BRIDE.

It was night—the night when Zalupah had promised to attempt to free his master; the night whem Alfrede had vowed to murder the helpless and unarmed prisoner.

Brackett was not yet asleep—seldom did sleep visit his eyes. He had just heard the sentinel for the mid-watch relieved, and was listening to his heavy footsteps as he paced to and fro before the dungeon door, when he heard the soldier hail some one who was approaching.—To the cry of "Who comes there?" the answer was given :

"A father of the church !"

The countersign was demanded and given, then the prisoner to his astonishment heard the new comer demand to be admitted to his cell. The sentinel, who played his part well, demanded the usual order; it was shown to him, and, apparently satisfied, the soldier opened the door to admit the holy "father of the church."

Brackett was about to demand the reason of this singular and untimely visit, when the stranger, who was indeed habited as a priest, whispered :—

"Be silent and on your guard. I am a friend !"

Thinking that he had heard the voice before, and that perchance this was some messenger from his bride, the ranger made no objection to the visi of the stranger, whose form he could but dimly distinguish by the feeble glimmering of his prison lamp.

As he rode rapidly up toward the enemy, with his truce-flag flinging out its white folds upon the breeze, Brackett saw another hoisted on a lance shaft in the columns of the enemy, and fearlessly rode up to it, while the Mexican columns came to a halt.

On inquiring who was the officer in command of the advance, Brackett learned to his joy that it was General Vasquez, and at once requested to be led to him.

As the general saw him, and the flag which was now his protection, he smiled, and frankly extending his hand, said—

"You were lucky in effecting your escape, brave cavalier, in time to take part in the struggle which must take place, for it would pain a soldier's heart to be held a helpless prisoner while his countrymen were upon the battle-field'."

"I believe I have to thank Colonel Alfrede for my liberty," replied the ranger, "and I hope that I shall soon have an opportunity to return my thanks upon the battle-field."

"You will, probably, but you have more to thank him for, than you are aware of!"

"Oh, it is more to curse him for, I fear!" replied the ranger, "my business here in your presence is to face him and force him to answer me one question."

"I know what your question would be, and thanks to him, are able to answer it!" said the general. "You seek your lost bride, and you seek not in vain."

"Oh, God! where is she? Is she safe, not in his power?"

"Safe, under my protection now, but shall be in your's soon."

The general gave an order to an aid—the officer rode back to the centre, and in a few moments returned with the beautiful Magdalena, who rode upon a mule. She was pale and faint with fatigue, but her face reddened with a rich glow of delight as she saw her beloved once more, and she flew to his arms with a wild cry of joy.

For a moment the two embraced in speechless happiness, then turning to their noble friend Vasquez, they poured out the expressions of their full hearts to him who had proved so nobly kind unto them. The gallant old soldier was almost as must excited as were they, and the great tears of pleasure rolled down his bronzed cheeks as he gazed upon their tender meeting.

"My mission is completed?" said Brackett a moment after—"I have found my bride, and must now return to my duty!"

"Go, and God's blessing follow thee!" exclaimed Vasquez, and then more saddly he added, "Send your bride far into the rear of your army, for ere another day, I fear that army will be on the retreat!"

"General Taylor does not know how to order a retreat; he may fall, his rmy may perish, but never will you see his back!" said the ranger proudly.

"I know that he is brave," replied Vasquez, "but we number five times more than his force. Our very weight must crush him!"

"Heavy weights are unwidely—the lightest men are the most active," replied the ranger with a smile.

"I fear that you will find us too much for you this time, and I fain would see blood spared, for life is precious to men—if your general would surrender Saltillo and fall back with his army, I could almost agree that he should not be pursued. Bear a message to him from me."

"Were I to bear a proposition to him for a surrender of one inch of ground which he has gained, he would drive me from his precence with scorn and contempt!" said Brackett.

"You Americans are very strange people. You never count numbers or cost, when you go into a fight. You seem to shut your eyes when you rush to the battle field!" said the old general.

"We always keep them open, when we are there!" rejoined the ranger, "but I must not longer delay. Once more thanking you for preserving my precious bride, I must take my leave. I pray that we at least may not meet upon the battle field hand to hand, and if we do, other foes shall receive my blows."

"And mine—but beware of Alfrede—he will be there, surrounded and followed by his desperate lancers—beware of being overpowered, for he is a fiend, and will fight now, for his hate is like a bursting volcano."

"I only ask that we may meet!" replied the ranger, then bowing low in his saddle to his courteous and magnanimous foe, he turned again his rein to the northward, bearing with him his now happy bride.

Darkness was again coming upon the earth, when he placed Magdalena in the arms of her father and sister, and then was forced again to part with her, for the distant firing told that the combat had already begun, and that soon the heavier shocks of a regular battle must follow. Therefore he at once hastened to the quarters of his general, whom he found surrounded with officers to whom he was giving his orders of battle.

The firing which the ranger had heard, was only the meeting of the outposts of the two armies, and the general knew that the actual ball would not open before morning. Yet now, under cover of the shadows of night he was forming his line to receive the foe, preparing with all his energy, to fight one of the most desperate battles that the pen of history has recorded since the days of Leonidas the Spartan.

"Well, sir, how many are they?" asked Taylor quickly, as his eye fell upon the ranger, who had joined the group of officers who surrounded him.

"Full twenty thousand, if I am to believe their own reports and my own observation."

"Just enough to give us a good day's work—we need exercise, I'm afraid we'll forget how to fight if we lay idle so long at a time!" said the old general with a smile. Such a smile and such tones as his were well calculated to reassure the hearts of his officers, some of whom felt that the odds between their five, and the enemy's twenty thousand men, were indeed desperate.

But it was not numbers, that the old General thought of, it was that he knew what kind of material his little army was composed of, which gave him the confidence to risk this battle.

"He had the surviving heroes of Palo Alto—Resaca de la Palma and Monterey, still with him—men whom he knew to be as true as the steel which they carried—men whom he had seen climbing the hills of Monterey amid the sheets of fire and storm of balls which thinned their ranks as the hail cuts down the green blades of the young corn—men who had with him endured heat and thirst and hunger, and the weary toils of the march, without a murmur, and he knew that they were invincible.

"I wish a thorough reconnoisance of the enemy's line, and a full description of the ground between them and our own lines, Captain Bracket!" said the old general, "you will perform this duty, and return to me as soon as possible. Your place to-morrow will be by my side."

The ranger hastened off to perform his duty, pausing but one instant to kiss the pale cheek of his virgin bride, and to bid her await fearlessly the result of the morrow's conflict.

And she—wept she when she saw him ride forth? Oh, no—a Spanish bride never sheds a coward tear when goes her lover, brother, or husband forth to battle.

She may pray on bended knees for his preservation and success, but she weeps not for his danger,

During all that long night the troops were moving about on Buena Vista, gaining in column and in line, by squadron and by company, the posts which their general had chosen.

Few eyes closed on that night—each motion was conducted in almost perfect silence. Calm and ominous seemed the stillness; it seemed as if the elements were suspending their usual duties to witness the fearful conflict which was soon to ensue. The wind moved not through the trees, or stirred a ripple on the silvery bosom of Juan's gentle river—neither rain nor thunder-cloud came to disturb the slumbers of such as chose to cast them down upon their arms, to wait in slumber for the tongue which with the dawn's early light was to awaken them—the hoarse tongue of battle.

Officers rode here and there, conveying orders to the different divisions, and thus ere the dawn of day came to light upon the battle-field, all was ready for the conflict.

There they stood, Washington's battery of the gallant fourth in the road which led to the south, the volunteer regiments to his right and left, the mounted men of Arkansas and Kentucky close at the mountain's base.

Thus with the narrow valley walled across with ardent and gallant men, the sun arose upon the field of Buena Vista on the 23d day of February, 1847.

CHAPTER XVII.

SUN-RISE UPON THE BATTLE FIELD. OLD ROUGH-AND-READY TAKES HIS POSITION.—A GENERAL VIEW OF THE ATTACK AND DEFENCE—CHARGE OF MAY —PERILOUS SITUATION OF BRACKETT AND HIS COMRADES.

THE day dawned upon the serried lines of both friend and foe, and while yet the grey of twilight was over them, the rattling of musketry along the mountain side to the left told that the combat was begun.

No. 8.

Loud cheers arose from every lip as "OLD ROUGH AND READY" took his station in the centre, and now began the fray in real earnest. Where a gun could be brought in play, its deadly fire was opened, and murmurs alone arose from those who had not yet been brought into a position to share in the conflict.

The sight was grand, terrific beyond the powers of description. The enemy's artillery had all opened their fire—their infantry were engaged in pouring in a deadly fire of musketry, and under cover of all this, his immense calvary force was preparing for the charge.

Meantime the eagle eye of Taylor was scanning all parts of the field. He saw now that the enemy were concentrating a force of cavalry at the base of the mountain, evidently intending to attack his waggon train and baggage, which was stationed near the ruined walls of Don Ignatio's former residence.

The eye of the general brightened. He turned to Brackett, who had been panting to join in the conflict, and cried, as he pointed to the cavalry of the enemy:

"Ride, sir, to May's position; the colonel has been foaming to make a charge; tell him that with his squadron, Bucker's company, and Pike's Arkansas boys, he must head off those lancers! You know the ground, you can show him the way!"

Oh, gladly leapt the heart of the young ranger then in his manly breast. He knew that his time for action had commenced, and he hoped to meet his marked foe among those lancers.

Driving his spurs deep into the flanks of his snorting steed he dashed off to the spot were May sat upon his large black horse, chafing madly at not receiving orders to join in the fray.

When he saw Brackett riding towards him in hot haste, his face brightened, for he felt that his general had "cut out some work" for him.

"Where now?" he asked as the ranger rode up to his side.

Quickly the general's orders were given; then, almost as quickly the squadrons were formed into column, and May shouting his usual cry, "Follow!" dashed on side by side with Brackett.

Soon the charge was heard from the Mexican bugles, and in a moment both masses of horsemen were dashing on at full speed, each to meet the other.

Oh, those were fearful sounds to hear—the shouts of the excited men, the groans of the wounded and dying; the yells of the wild horsemen of the west. Clash of steel, and pistol shots; the cries of wounded horses; the crashing of heavy sabres as down they clove through flesh and bone; oh, these indeed, were fearful sounds.

On—on, wheeling in pursuit of the broken squadrons of the enemy rushed the American horsemen; and close in the rear of the squadrons of Alfrede, which again had turned and fled, rode Brackett, supported by a few of his own rangers and some gallant Kentuckians, not more than twenty in all. He was fast gaining upon the flying lancers, and his voice reached the ears of his foe as he fled.

Casting back a hasty glance, Alfrede saw how few were the men who were with the ranger, and he began to blush at flying with five hundred lancers from so few. Giving the order to wheel, he suddenly swept around with his squadrons, and in a moment had completely encircled the little band, and now closed around them, separating them entirely from the rest of their force, and hiding them from the view of their busy comrades, in the cloud of dust, and by his superior numbers,

www.ingramcontent.com/pod-product-compliance
Lightning Source LLC
Chambersburg PA
CBHW081215170626
46811CB00010B/3301